The Case Files of
Young Master Detective Brooke Alans:

The Mysterious Disappearance
at
Bloomington River

By: Sarah Rivera

Made For More Publishing LLC

The Mysterious Disappearance at Bloomington River
A Mystery Series for Young Detectives

The Case Files of Young Master Detective Brooke Alans

Library of Congress Control Number: 2025908215
Paperback ISBN: 979-8-9987508-1-6
Hardback ISBN: 979-8-9987508-0-9

Published by: Made For More Publishing LLC
                Colcord, OK
Edited by: Naomi Books, LLC
Printed in the United States of America

Dedication

Dedicated with love to my mom, Laura Beachy,
for helping me have this story turned into a *real* book.
You don't know how much all your hard work means to me.

Contents

Prologue

Turning to look at her friend and her brother, Brooke asked, "Are you guys ready to solve our first case?" She was clearly excited!

Thomas responded first, "You bet we are! We've been waiting for the big reveal, and now we get to hear it!"

Brooke looked at Evan next, and he nodded. "Yeah! I can't wait to see their faces when they find out who the culprit is!"

"Or culprits," Thomas added.

The door to the mayor's office swung open just as they approached. The mayor stood there in front of them.

"Oh, there you are. I was wondering when you were going to get here." He looked at each of them in turn. "The receptionist told me you were on your way."

Mayor Andrews stepped back from the doorway and motioned for them to come in. "Alright," he said. "You can begin whenever you're ready."

Everyone stared expectantly at Brooke.

"I assume you've cracked the case. Isn't that why we're all here?" Mayor Andrews asked, gesturing around with his hands at the people she had invited.

Brooke smiled and looked first at Evan, then at Thomas. Finally, she looked directly at the mayor.

"Yes, I have, Mayor Andrews, and you are *not* going to believe me when I tell you what *really* happened."

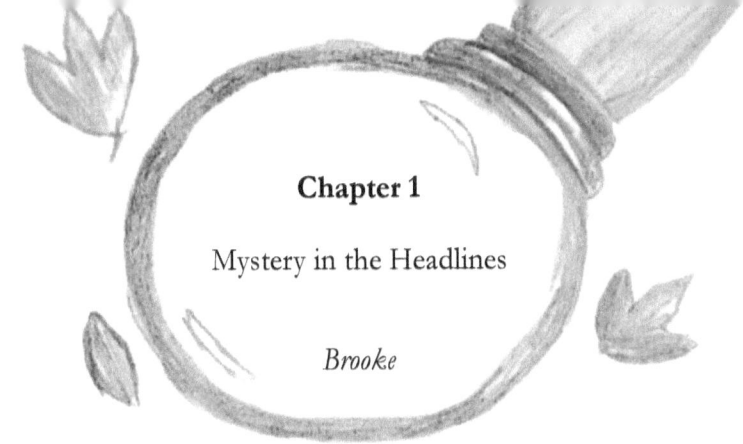

Chapter 1

Mystery in the Headlines

Brooke

Y ES! BROOKE GLANCED at the alarm clock with its bright blue light, reading 6:30 a.m. She had finally woken up on time! Climbing out of bed, she first went to open the blinds, the sunlight beaming down on her as if in congratulations. Going to her closet and then her dresser, Brooke picked out her clothes and headed to the bathroom to change. Afterward, she brushed her hair and snatched up her books from her desk. She had just loaded everything into her bag when the alarm clock beeped.

Brooke looked at the clock, then made her way over and turned off the alarm. She thought to herself, *I'm at least thirty minutes ahead!* She picked up her backpack from her desk and went downstairs. On her way, she passed by her older brother Evan and gave him a quick wave before proceeding down.

Upon entering the living room, Brooke immediately smelled the delicious aroma of French toast and eggs.

"Breakfast is ready, sleepyheads!" called their mom from the kitchen. Brooke entered the kitchen and sat at the table right before her mom placed a plate of food in front of her.

Brooke's brother soon joined her at the table, and after they both prayed, they ate their breakfast. After putting her dish in the sink and drinking her orange juice, she picked up her bag and started toward the door.

Her mother called from inside the kitchen, "In case you're wondering where Dad is, he went to work early. He had an important business meeting, and he didn't want to be late for it."

Brooke put on her shoes and opened the door. "Alright, I'll see you later. Bye, Mom!"

She stepped outside and was greeted by a lovely autumn day as she walked down the sidewalk to the bus stop. It was nice, not too chilly, and there was a slight breeze in the air. The leaves on every tree were also turning a lovely shade of amber and orange and looked almost like they were straight out of a painting.

On her way to the bus stop, she passed Miss Dearlee's house. Miss Dearlee was a kind old woman who made them Christmas cookies every year and almost always knitted something special for each of them. Aside from that, she also owned a few pets, one of them being a black-and-white cat named Oreo that recently had kittens. Miss Dearlee had let Brooke name one of them, so she chose the one that was white and fluffy. The kitten had one blue eye and one green, and she named her Jewel.

Often, Jewel would play in the backyard with her siblings and let Brooke pet her when she passed by to get to the bus stop. But today, Jewel must have been inside because, as far as Brooke could tell, no kittens were in the yard. She continued walking and eventually made it to the bus stop. Shortly after, the bus arrived, and she got on and found a seat.

Unfortunately, none of her friends took the same bus to school, so she usually sat by herself. Looking out the window, they passed house after house, turned onto street after street, until finally they arrived at the school building. Once the bus came to a stop, she stood up, grabbed her bag, then headed toward the school doors.

Her friends Casey and Mable greeted and joined her, and they started toward their classroom.

"So, how was your weekend, Brooke?" asked Casey, turning to look at her friend.

"Pretty good. I told you guys about the kittens, right? They're super adorable, and I got to name one. If it weren't for my mom's allergy to fur, I'd probably be able to keep one too."

Casey laughed. "Yeah, you already told us about them last week when they were just born. It seems like that's all you ever talk about."

"Yeah, you should talk about other things too," Mable joked.

Suddenly, Casey spoke up in a more serious tone, "Did you guys read the newspaper they passed out today?"

Mable and Brooke exchanged glances, and Brooke replied, "I haven't yet. Why?"

Casey looked at them both and responded, "Well, it says that over in New York, some little girl fell into a river and was swept downstream. A few officers have looked for her, but so far, they haven't found her body. Isn't that a little odd?"

"Odd that someone fell into a river in a busy place like New York, or odd that they couldn't find her body?" Mable asked.

"Well, both, I guess, but I was talking about the fact that they couldn't find the body," Casey replied.

The bell went off at that moment, and the girls hurried down the hall. Casey and Mable rushed into the classroom.

Before entering, Brooke told them, "I'll meet you there in a second. I wanna go check something."

Mable and Casey nodded, and Brooke hurried down the hall. Once she went through the large double doors of the school building, she saw exactly what she was looking for—the newspaper stand! She hurried to it and grabbed a paper. Sure enough, after flipping through a few pages, she found the news article.

Young Girl Falls into Bloomington River

At 4:37 p.m. on November 17th, young, nine-year-old Julie Rosette Peters was washed downstream after allegedly jumping into the Bloomington River near Montgomery Lane. After a brief investigation of the scene and a search of the river, officials were unable to find the girl or recover her body.

After speaking to a few witnesses, officials suggested the possibility that young Julie was pushed into the river rather than having jumped in herself. With the current having been particularly strong that day, officials unfortunately believe the girl is most likely dead. Further investigation will continue to locate her body.

After reading the story, Brooke put the paper in her backpack and went back inside. She hurried back toward the classroom, almost completely lost in her thoughts as she rushed down the hall. *Casey's right: it is a little odd that they haven't found the body. The Bloomington River hits a piece of land before going to the ocean. So, if anything were washed down the river, it would end up there. So, why haven't they found her yet?*

It was pretty clear the officials didn't know if Julie was alive or not, which led to the question: "If she was alive, then where was she?" She couldn't just disappear. While there was always the possibility that she could have just *fallen* into the river, Brooke doubted it.

Well, one thing was for certain: they weren't telling everything. Either that or something was off because things certainly did *not* seem right. Well, lucky for them, Brooke Alans was on the case, determined to figure out *The Mysterious Disappearance at Bloomington River.*

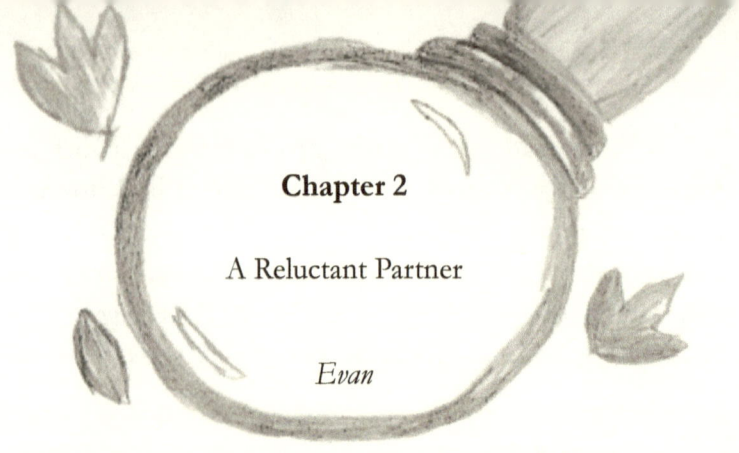

Chapter 2

A Reluctant Partner

Evan

"NOOOO!"

Evan woke up with a start, glaring at his alarm clock. This had to be the fourth time it had woken him up this morning, and each time he had snoozed it. Although *this* time, looking at the clock rather than snoozing it, he jumped out of bed and ran to get ready for school.

Evan usually got up early in the morning… at least most of the time. Okay, he *usually* got up just as the alarm went off, but it was better than being late.

He rushed to throw on his clothes, gather his books, and grab his backpack. Just then, the alarm clock went off again, but Evan didn't bother to shut it off. Instead, he put his bag on his back and left the room.

On his way down the hall, he saw his sister. She must have gotten up before him, judging by the fact that she was already dressed and heading downstairs. She waved a quick hello to him as she passed by.

He could smell Mom's breakfast cooking. It was always great whenever she made his favorite blueberry muffins, but he could tell by the smell in the air that she had made French toast and eggs instead. Well, that wasn't too bad either. Mom's food was always delicious.

Evan took a seat at the table across from his sister as his mom placed a yummy-smelling plate of food in front of him. After he and Brooke prayed, they ate breakfast and prepared to leave for school.

Brooke was up from the table first. She put her dish in the sink and headed out the door. Evan did the same and said goodbye to his mom before leaving. Brooke normally took the bus to school, so she walked in the opposite direction from Evan. Evan went toward the driveway; he often drove himself to school rather than taking the bus. Being the older sibling had its advantages, and that meant he got to drive a car before Brooke. Even though he was only two years older than her, it made all the difference to him.

Getting in the car, he started the engine and drove off to school. Sometimes, he would take shortcuts on purpose just to get to school before the bus and beat Brooke there. Today, he just drove to school on the main roads, thinking about the math assessment he was supposed to take once he got there. The longer it took him to get to school, the longer it would be before he had to take that test.

Eventually, he turned into the school parking lot and slid into an open space. As he entered the building, he noticed his friend Ethan. When he walked up to him, he saw Ethan was already talking to a few younger boys.

"And then, the swamp monster came up, grabbed her, and pulled her into the water. She was taken downstream, never to be seen again!" Ethan said, in his best storytelling voice, as the younger kids stared at him.

"What are you talking about?" Evan asked.

Ethan looked at him as if just noticing he was there and replied, "Hey dude, you're late. You just missed it. I was telling them the story about how that swamp monster from the newspaper pulled that girl into the river!"

Evan looked a little confused at first and then laughed. "Must have been a scary monster, but what was that part you mentioned about the newspaper?"

Just then, Evan's other friend Clara walked over.

"Ignore him. He's just trying to scare those kids," she said, handing something to Evan. "Some parts of what he said were true, though, and it's in the newspaper if you wanna check it out."

Evan took the newspaper just as Ethan replied, "Yeah, see! Some of what I said *was* true. There might be swamp monsters hanging out in that river."

Clara turned back to Evan and replied, "*Not* the swamp monster part."

Looking through the paper, and after turning a few pages, he found the story about a kid named Julie who had jumped into the river. *So, what's so great about that?* He thought to himself. Then he kept reading. It seemed a little weird that they didn't find her body, but other than that, it was just another matter for the police to deal with. It was also all the way over in New York, which was an hour's drive from here, so why would it concern him?

Handing the paper back to Clara, who was still arguing with Ethan about swamp monsters, Evan replied jokingly, "Interesting! For some reason, they left out the part about monsters."

Ethan and Clara both turned to look at him.

Ethan laughed and said, "Yeah."

Clara just rolled her eyes. The bell rang, so they all hurried down the hall.

"What class do you guys have first?" Ethan asked the other two.

"I have Social Studies first," said Clara.

"What about you, Evan?"

"I've got…um…" It took Evan a second to recall what class he had, but then he remembered with a gasp. "Oh, no! I've got math, and we've got a test today!"

He started rushing down the hallway. "I'll catch up with you guys later! Bye!"

"See you at lunch!" Clara called after him as he rounded the corner.

Evan rushed to the classroom as fast as he could without running in the hall. When he made it to class, he hurried to his seat and got there just seconds before the teacher entered the room. Setting his bag down, he got out his notebook and got ready for the test.

* * * * *

After many long hours of classes, Evan finally heard the bell ring again. Picking up his bag and leaving the classroom, he headed down the hall to join his friends for lunch. On his way into the cafeteria, he bumped into Brooke.

"Hey, so how did your test go?" she asked.

"Pretty good. I think I got an A." Then Evan's expression changed to confusion. "Wait, how did you know I took a test?"

"Clara told me. I saw her on my way to lunch," Brooke responded, shrugging. "Also, I wanted to tell you something."

Evan asked curiously, "What is it?"

Brooke replied, "Come on, I'll tell you during lunch."

At the nearest empty table, Brooke and Evan sat down and opened their lunches. After taking a bite of his peanut butter-and-jelly sandwich, he asked, "So, what is it?"

Brooke took something out of her bag and placed it in the middle of the table.

"A newspaper?"

Brooke gave a quick nod and asked, "Yep. Did you read the story about..."

Evan cut her off. "About the girl who fell in the river? Yeah. Clara showed it to me this morning. What about it?"

Brooke looked at him with an expression that made him wonder if he had asked something dumb. "What do you mean, what about it? It's a mystery!" Brooke said excitedly.

Taking another bite of his sandwich, he asked, "What makes you think that?"

"You don't get it, do you? The article says that the girl was washed downstream, right?"

"Right," was Evan's response.

She questioned him again. "Okay, well, they also said they haven't found her and don't know if she's dead or alive, right?"

"Um, yeah. Where is this going?" he asked with a puzzled look on his face.

"Hang on, I'm getting to it," Brooke replied with a little annoyance.

She continued, "So, they don't know if she's dead or alive, and they haven't found her body. If you remember the time when Mom gave us that quiz on geography, then you'll remember that the Bloomington River in New York leads to the ocean, and before it goes into the ocean, it hits a little bit of land," Brooke explained.

Evan sat up. "Yeah," he said. "On the land before the river, right?" He was starting to understand where his sister was going with all this.

"So then, she should have been found by now!" he exclaimed.

"Exactly!" Brooke said, beaming. "So, then, *that* would mean there's a possibility she's still alive since they haven't found her yet."

"You're right," Evan said. "Good detective work!"

"Thanks! So now, I plan to go down to the Bloomington River and try to solve this mystery."

Evan's expression immediately changed. "What do you mean *you're* going to solve the mystery? You can't just declare to Mom and Dad that you're going to New York to look for a possible ghost!"

"I don't know *how* yet, but I *am* going to solve this mystery. Also, they never said she was dead." Brooke replied.

"Even so, you shouldn't go," he said. "Remember what the newspaper article said? It said someone may have pushed her into the river, and if you go looking for her, the culprit won't want to be found. So, most likely, they'll want to push *you* into the river, too!" Evan stared at his sister in disbelief.

Brooke protested with a wave of her hand. "Oh, I doubt it. How's anyone even gonna know that's what I'm looking for? People go to New York all the time—to do a lot of different things."

Evan was starting to get upset that his younger sister wasn't understanding what he was saying. "People will figure it out as soon as you start asking questions!"

Brooke raised her voice. "Why don't you ever agree with me?"

Running out of things to say to convince her not to go, Evan didn't respond right away. As he was about to speak again, Ethan came up to their table.

"Oh, hey, Brooke! Have you heard about the girl who jumped in the river? There's a story about it in the newspaper."

Brooke just glared at him.

Evan responded, "That's what we were just talking about."

It didn't take long for Ethan to get the hint that they were in the middle of a heated conversation, so without another word, he went back to his table.

Turning his attention back to his sister, Evan spoke again. "I don't understand why you don't get it. Going out and doing detective work is not smart. Once people figure out you're trying to solve a case…"

"Mystery," Brooke interrupted.

Evan continued, "*Whatever* it is, they won't be happy that you're trying to figure out what happened. Haven't you watched any movies or anything lately? That's how it always ends up!"

"You worry too much. I'm still going," Brooke said, glaring at him. "And you can't change my mind."

Chapter 3

Brooke Lucks Out

Brooke

B ROOKE PICKED UP her backpack and got up from the table, purposely leaving the newspaper where her brother could see it. Thinking there was nothing more to say, she began walking to the table where Mable and Casey were sitting. She figured they would agree with her that it was cool to try to figure out the mystery. As a matter of fact, Casey loved math and puzzles, and she would probably offer to help solve the case.

As she walked toward their table, Evan called after her, "Fine! But I'm coming with you."

Brooke turned and looked at him, still a little upset about their earlier conversation. "Really? What about you saying it's not a good idea?"

Evan immediately responded, "It's not, and I still think that. But you can't go clue hunting on your own."

She stepped back to the table and picked up the newspaper she had left there. She glanced at Evan just in time to catch a smile.

"And who knows? It might be kinda fun," he said, shrugging a little.

She smiled back before walking away.

Mable glanced at Brooke's brother and then back at her before asking, "So, what was going on with you two?"

Brooke said, "Evan didn't want me to do detective work… but it's okay now."

"Detective work?" asked Mable, a little confused, although her expression quickly changed from concerned to excited. She noticed the newspaper in Brooke's hand. "You're going to try to figure out what happened to that girl from the paper, aren't you?"

Brooke answered excitedly. "Yep! Evan agreed to help me, too!"

"That's so cool!" Casey added.

They had just a few minutes to question Brooke, and then the bell rang.

Brooke stood and picked up her lunchbox. "We better get to class."

She waited for her friends to put their trays away, and then they all left the cafeteria together.

* * * * *

Brooke sat on the bus, waiting for her stop. Staring out the window and watching the trees pass by, she couldn't help but think about the mystery. She *was* going to solve it; she had no doubt about that. What she was wondering, though, was how in the world she would get to New York.

New York was more than an hour away from where they lived, even if it was "just across the border." Her parents would never let her go that far away, especially to solve a mystery. She tried to think of other ways to solve the case, but nothing seemed like it would work without her going.

Thinking about this, she lost track of time. By the time she noticed, the bus was already rolling down the street and close to her stop. Getting off the bus, Brooke tried to put thoughts of New York aside and think about other things. *Maybe if I stop focusing on things, it'll clear my mind, and then I'll find an answer.* At least that's what she figured, anyway.

She walked up the porch steps and was greeted by her brother, who had gotten to the house first. She wanted to go over to him right away so they could discuss how they would start working on the case. However, almost as soon as she entered the house, their mother came to them and began talking.

"I bet you two were wondering why your father had gone to work so early this morning," she said.

"Being the governor and all, he had to attend an important meeting. At this meeting, they decided they needed to speak to the mayor of New York City, and everyone felt your father should go there to speak with him. With that being said, your father decided to go to that meeting in New York tomorrow."

She continued, looking at Brooke and Evan. "Since you two have never been to New York, I thought you might like to go with your dad. So, what do you guys think?"

Brooke's face immediately lit up. This was exactly what she needed! Now, she'd have a way to get to New York to work on the case!

"I'll go!" she said to her mother, trying not to sound too excited. She snuck a glance at Evan, hoping he'd get the hint, too.

He replied, "Yeah, I'll go too."

Their mother responded with a nod. "Alright then. Go let your father know, then start packing."

As she went up the stairs, Brooke couldn't believe how she had lucked out! Hurrying down the hallway, she noticed Evan wasn't following her, so she assumed he was already packing.

Brooke found her dad sitting at the computer in the upstairs study. Once she entered the room, he looked up and said, "So, I assume your mother told you about the trip to New York?"

"Yep, and Evan and I want to go, too," Brooke answered with a nod.

Her dad replied with a smile, "Alright, it'll be fun to visit somewhere new with you kids. You better get to packing," he said before turning back to the computer.

Brooke left the study, but once she got to the stairs, she called back to her father, "When are we leaving?"

She heard him yell from the other room, "We'll be leaving tomorrow at twelve o'clock, so be ready!"

"Alright!" she yelled back before going downstairs to her brother's room.

She knocked and called, "We're leaving at noon tomorrow! Make sure you're packing!"

"I plan on it," came the slightly irritated response from her brother.

Back upstairs once again, she went into her room. As she walked toward her desk, she noticed a dark blue, fairly large plastic suitcase sitting by the chair. She assumed her mother had placed it there for her to use, so she lifted it up and plopped it down on the bed.

Opening it, she wondered what she would need to bring. Her mind immediately went to necessities, so she piled some clothes, a toothbrush, a hairbrush, and a few other items into the suitcase. Then she started to think about the kind of things she might need to solve the mystery. From her desk, she grabbed a notebook and pencil and put them in the suitcase as well. Just in case, she also threw in her camera, a flashlight, and a magnifying glass. Every detective had a magnifying glass!

Doing a final check for anything else that might help, she went to her closet. The only things she found there were clothes and shoes, but nothing useful for solving mysteries. So, instead, she returned to the suitcase, which looked surprisingly full for the few clothes and necessities loaded into it, and she zipped it closed. Brooke lugged the suitcase from her room and down the stairs. She left it by the front door and then went to say goodnight to her mother.

After changing into her pajamas, she got into bed and tried to fall asleep, but she couldn't help thinking things through. It had definitely worked out great that her dad happened to be going to New York. It was even better that he had offered to take them along, although the main, or only, reason her father was going was for his business meetings. Most likely, while he was in meetings, she and Evan would have plenty of time to check out the scene of the mystery and do some sleuthing.

All the thinking seemed to finally wear her out because she slowly drifted off and dreamed of how she'd soon be solving a *real* case… like a true detective.

Chapter 4

The Adventure Begins

Brooke

"WAKE UP, SLEEPYHEAD!" Brooke's dad called from her bedroom door.

She sat up in bed sleepily and looked through her open doorway. Her father was walking down the hallway to his own room, and she could see that he was already dressed for his business meeting. Guessing he just wanted to make sure she had everything ready to go and that there was no rush yet, she laid back down and stared at the ceiling. There was no point in trying to fall back asleep now. Sunlight poured in from the sides of the curtains, landing on her face and signaling that it was daytime.

She sat back up and glanced curiously at her alarm clock. Squinting her eyes against the sun, she read the time.

"Eleven-thirty. Okay," she mumbled sleepily.

Suddenly, she realized what she had just said aloud. She had to look at the clock again!

"Wait... eleven-thirty!"

Brooke jumped out of bed and rushed to get changed. She was supposed to be leaving with her dad and brother at twelve! Throwing on clothes and gathering a few last-minute items, she ran down the stairs.

Brooke dashed into the kitchen, where she saw her mom getting their lunches ready.

"Good, you're up. I told your father to go get you. I thought I'd let you sleep in a bit, but it was starting to get late. You don't want to make your father have to wait on you."

Brooke nodded, made herself a bowl of cereal, and sat down at the table. After she finished eating, she checked the time on the microwave clock. It read 11:58, so she figured any second now, her dad would tell them it was time to go, and they would head out to the car. She had just enough time to get her suitcase so she would be ready.

As she reached for it, her dad came down the stairs with his own suitcase.

"As if on cue," Brooke joked.

"Alright, kids, let's load up!" her dad said. He walked toward the garage door.

Evan yelled, "Coming!"

Brooke watched him rush toward them, carrying a big backpack instead of a suitcase.

After their things were placed in the trunk, Dad said, "Alright. Is everyone ready to go?"

"Yep!" Brooke and Evan replied in unison.

Mom came out and gave them each a hug and made sure they had packed everything they needed. After several goodbyes, she finally went back inside, and they got ready to leave.

Evan ran to the passenger side door. "I call sitting in the front!"

"You can't call it!" Brooke yelled after him, running to beat him there. He got to the door just a second before she did and sat down in the passenger seat with a satisfied smile.

Rolling her eyes at her brother, Brooke slid into the back seat. Dad got in, everyone buckled up, and they set off for New York City. Looking out her window, Brooke tried to think of something to do as they rode.

It would be an hour and a half before they got there, so she knew she had to think of something because it was a long car ride. Looking around, first inside the car, then outside, she found nothing interesting.

After a while, she thought of two possible things she could do. One was to take a nap, which was the most obvious. The other was to talk to pass the time, even though she knew she wouldn't be able to hold a conversation for longer than a few minutes. Between the two, she decided on talking. At least it was better than taking a nap.

Looking at her dad through the rearview mirror, she asked,

"So, how long of a drive is it?" She already knew how long it would be but couldn't think of any other questions to ask, so she went with that.

"Probably an hour and a half," came her dad's response. "Maybe longer or shorter. It depends on traffic."

"Yeah," Evan said, turning around to speak to Brooke, "and it also depends on how many bathroom breaks you need to take." He gave her a sarcastic smile before going back to his phone.

Brooke rolled her eyes at her brother's remark. Turning back to her dad, she tried to think of something else to say to pass the time, but she couldn't think of anything. *Well, that was the end of that conversation*, Brooke thought to herself. That had to be her new record for the shortest conversation ever.

Looking back out the window, she watched each car go by. Then she focused on the trees they passed. Staring out the window wasn't *that* bad, considering there was a little scenery, even if she *had* seen it a dozen times. She kept watching as long as she could until she felt tired. Her eyes began to close, and soon enough, she was fast asleep with her head against the window.

* * * * *

The car suddenly hit a bump, and Brooke woke up. She looked around, quickly remembering they were in the car, still on their way to New York. Glancing out the window, she noticed the change in scenery. Buildings had replaced all the trees, and in place of country mountains were tall towers that blocked any glimpse of a scenic view.

Once they drove onto the busy streets, it was clearly different from her hometown. There were electronic billboards on buildings everywhere. Most people looked as if they were in such a rush to get somewhere, and hardly a regular car was in sight—all replaced by taxis.

As they continued driving, this remained the view for quite a while until, eventually, they pulled onto a side road that led to rows of giant houses. Brooke looked at each one, trying to guess which house was where they'd be staying. That was one of the fun things about going with Dad on business trips. They always got to stay in new places. Whether it be a new house or a new state, it was always fun.

Besides that, since her dad was the governor of their state, whenever he traveled for meetings, they would often provide a very nice place for him to stay. Often, it was a big house, which was always fun for her and Evan to explore and play hide-and-seek in, even if that was something younger kids would do.

The car began slowing down, and finally, they turned into a driveway. As her dad parked, Brooke leaned her head out the window to get a better view. The house had white brick walls, and all the shutters were painted black. Upon further inspection, the house looked a lot like an old Victorian home, just updated to look nicer and more modern.

Once the car was parked, Brooke got out and unloaded her suitcase from the trunk. Dragging it up the porch steps, she waited while her dad input the number combination on the automatic lock. Once finished, he swung the door open, and Brooke stepped inside. Since she had thought the outside looked nice, she was really taken aback by the inside. She would agree that the outside of the house looked huge compared to most houses, but the inside seemed even bigger, almost like a mansion.

It was even nicer than the outside, and everything was either white or a shade of gray, giving it that fancy but welcoming feel. Setting her suitcase down in the large entry room, she looked around. As soon as she proceeded to the next room, she was greeted by two large staircases at the far end, starting at different sides but meeting up at the top. In the center, between the staircases, there was a white brick fireplace with a television hanging above it. In the center of the room were a few light gray couches and some fluffy white rugs. She guessed this was supposed to be the living room.

Although Brooke was eager to explore upstairs first, she decided to go one floor at a time. Liking the idea of going around in order, she opened the first door to a room that appeared to be a bedroom. It seemed like a regular room compared to the rest of the house, but after a closer look, Brooke found a remote that made the ceiling cover slide back to reveal what she thought was a skylight—except it wasn't *exactly* a skylight. Above the glass, on the other side, were tropical fish swimming around! It was like a giant fish tank built into the ceiling, and it appeared to be completely filled with water. *An aquarium! Wow!* Thinking this was absolutely cool, she chose *this* room as the one she'd be staying in. She was "calling" this room. Evan could forget about it. She would bring her suitcase in later after her exploration was over for the night.

The next door was locked, so she assumed it was a storage room or where the water pipes or heater were installed. Moving back into the living room, she looked toward the front door. Dad was locking up the car, and Evan was bringing the last suitcase in. Since they both looked like they were still busy, she figured she had a little bit more time to explore.

The last areas to check were upstairs, so up she went. Most of the doors opened to normal rooms, like bedrooms, game rooms, and things like that. But two specific rooms happened to catch her eye. One appeared to be a study or an old parlor type of area. It was like the bedroom she'd chosen, except the floor was made of thick glass, and the fish swam under the room instead of above it. There was a TV in there as well, and a bunch of bookshelves that completed the "study room" feel.

As Brooke explored, another bedroom caught her attention. This one was slightly larger and nicer than the other one, in her opinion. It had a huge bed with one of those veil-looking things hanging from the ceiling above it and a big TV hanging from the wall at one end of the room. The carpet was super soft, and the walk-in closet was huge!

Brooke's favorite thing, though, was probably the windows. There were two grand windows at the far end of the room that were curved at the top. Going up to them for a closer look, she saw that these windows were actually doors that led outside. She pushed them open and stepped out onto a balcony that wrapped around the back of the house.

From the balcony, she could see the yard, pool, and flower garden. Overall, the place was *very* nice, and Brooke knew she would enjoy staying there until they returned home. After stepping back inside the room, she decided the balcony was too beautiful to resist, so she made a quick trip to get her suitcase and pulled it into the room. *Oh well. Evan may get the cool room with the fish in the ceiling, but I'm getting the room with the balcony. I call this one instead.*

Brooke took one final look around before returning to the second floor. She realized she had been so caught up with this place that she had completely forgotten about the mystery. Well, not *completely* forgotten; it was always in the back of her mind. This beautiful house had been a wonderful distraction, though, and a fun way to pass some time. Now, looking out the window, she could see the sun was starting to go down. There wouldn't be time to get around to any detective work today. But nothing was stopping her from it tomorrow!

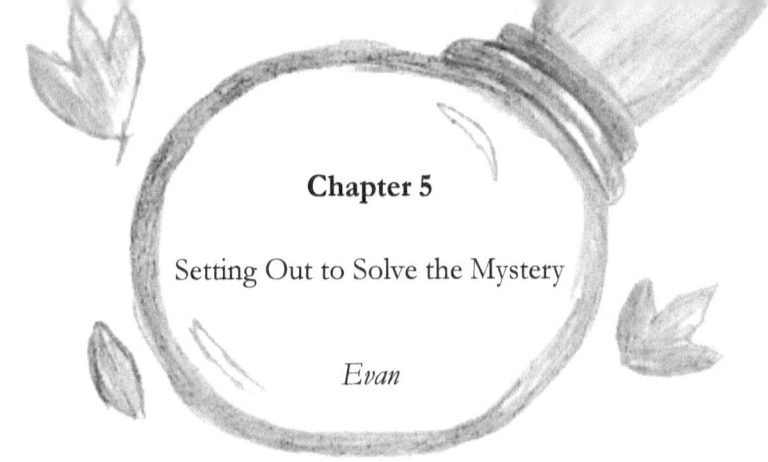

Chapter 5

Setting Out to Solve the Mystery

Evan

E VAN YAWNED as he sat up in bed. The alarm clock read 8:33, so he figured his sister would come charging into his room any time now, saying they should go look for clues to solve the mystery.

He blinked, trying to wake himself up as he looked around. It had taken him a second to realize where he was. After one glance up at the ceiling, he quickly remembered. The multi-colored fish swam as if taking no notice of him, swimming off in all different directions in the glass tank above him. He didn't know who had the idea of designing a ceiling like that; he just hoped it wouldn't break while he was sleeping.

After changing, he found Brooke sitting in the living room with her notebook. Walking over, he asked, "Ready to solve a mystery?"

Brooke happily responded, "Yep! We'll have plenty of time, too. While Dad's at his meeting, we have all day to look around here and see if we can find anything that will help."

Evan agreed and went into the kitchen for breakfast. After eating, he and Brooke headed out. Walking down the sidewalk, it didn't seem like they were in New York. There were no billboards or vast crowds, just a bunch of houses like back in their neighborhood. The only difference was that the houses here were bigger, and the occasional taxi passed by.

Once they had finally walked out of the rows of houses, they approached the city area, and then it started to look and feel a lot more like New York City. They stopped to wait to cross the road with several other people, and they noticed all the different advertisements. There were a bunch of electronic billboards, signs, and posters on shop windows, and pieces of paper that were taped to trees and metal poles. People here clearly liked to advertise.

Once the light turned red for the cars, they crossed the road. It was about this time that Evan realized they hadn't really been heading anywhere specific, so he stopped to ask his sister, "Where are we going?"

She responded, "I'm heading to the river from the newspaper article." Then she kept walking.

Catching up to her, Evan asked, "And do you know where that is?"

"Nope, but I saw it from the picture in the paper, so I'll know it when I see it," Brooke said.

Evan wasn't so sure about that, and he definitely didn't want to get lost in such an enormous place. So, at the next newspaper stand, he walked up to the person behind the table and asked if he had any copies of yesterday's paper. The man looked a little confused but bent down and searched through some boxes. After fumbling through the contents for a while, he finally pulled out yesterday's newspaper and handed it to them. Evan thanked the man, paid for it, and he and Brooke continued walking.

Looking at her brother, a little confused, she asked, "Why'd you need a newspaper from yesterday?"

Evan replied, "So we could find wherever we're trying to get to. I don't want to be on a wild goose chase."

He flipped to the article and pointed. "Look, it says it happened at Bloomington River, wherever that is, and it was near Montgomery Lane."

Brooke nodded. "Now we just need to figure out where those places are."

He handed the newspaper to her. "You could probably ask someone for directions."

"Really? Ask who? Everyone's in a rush to get somewhere and will probably just ignore us," Brooke said, taking the paper and looking down at it.

Evan shrugged and looked around. She was right; unless they found some directions, they'd probably be wandering around for hours.

Unfortunately, that was exactly what ended up happening. It had been almost two hours, and they hadn't found anything that looked even remotely close to the picture in the newspaper. After walking around for what seemed like forever, Brooke stopped in front of Evan and spoke.

"Okay, you were right. We need to find someone who can give us directions. We've been out here for hours, and I don't want to keep going in circles."

Evan was tempted to say, "I told you so," but why bother? It wouldn't help them find the Bloomington River. They started toward the first shop on this street, hoping that whoever was working there would have time to give them directions. They walked across the street and made it just before a few more taxis raced by.

Just as Evan was about to open the door to the shop, he heard Brooke yell, "Hey Evan, look at that!"

He looked to see what she was pointing at. The poster, taped to a tree, read:

The Cherryton Festival is now open!
The annual Cherryton Festival will be open
Monday through Wednesday, from 9:00
am–8:00 pm. This year, the festival is being
held on Montgomery Lane, near
Worthington Park.

Hope you can join us!

Evan realized why Brooke had pointed at the poster. *They were trying to get to Montgomery Lane!*

"So, if we find the festival, we'll find the location of the disappearance!"

"Exactly!" Brooke replied, running ahead. "Come on, let's head over there!"

Now that they knew they were looking for a festival, it wasn't so hard to find. All they needed to do was look for signs, booths, lights, and people. Looking ahead, they noticed more posters for the Cherryton Festival. They followed along until they finally arrived at the festival entrance. There, the street sign at the corner confirmed that this was Montgomery Lane.

Evan looked around, not sure of what exactly to look for. They knew they should be close to the river, but there was no water in sight. Walking through the festival, they continued searching.

"We've been in the right place looking, and we haven't found it yet," Evan said.

"Yeah," Brooke said. "It's a fairly good-sized river, so you'd think we would have found it by now."

Evan looked at the street signs as they passed to keep an eye out for the river. After a while, he said to Brooke, "They should have more signs out around here, like they had back where we had to cross the street." He joked, "It's almost like they don't *want* us to find it."

They kept walking. Evan looked over at his sister and thought about what he had just said. Glancing around at every street sign they passed, he wondered if what he said was true. It was the area of a previous crime scene, so to speak. *What if they had the area restricted and purposely made it so no one could get there, let alone find it?* Although it did seem odd that no signs were pointing them toward the river, there had to be at least one out there somewhere. Shrugging off the thought, he examined the newspaper again. He was probably just being paranoid about it, anyway.

As they continued walking, they each kept an eye out for street signs or any other signs directing them toward the river. They were so busy searching that Evan almost didn't notice the river until it was right under his nose.

Chapter 6

A Close Call by the River

Brooke

"E VAN!" BROOKE CALLED, running to catch her brother. She ended up grabbing him by the back of his shirt as he dangled, with one foot barely on the river's edge and both arms flailing.

Evan hadn't been watching where he was going and had ended up slipping much too close to the river. Now, he was trying to regain his footing on the riverbank and keep himself from falling into the water.

"Stop moving! You're making it very hard for me to pull you back!" Brooke said, grunting as she tried to tug her brother away from the edge.

Irritable but frightened, she asked, "Why do you have to be so heavy?"

After what seemed like forever, Brooke was finally able to pull Evan backward onto solid ground and away from the river's edge. He sat down hard, breathing fast, and stared into the river. The water was moving rapidly, and it seemed that anything that fell into it would have been swept away at once.

"Brooke," he said, "Thanks! You'd think they'd have a railing or something to keep people from falling in!"

"Yeah, you'd think so," Brooke agreed before turning her attention to the river. He was right; there wasn't any railing or barrier to keep anything or anyone from falling in. She stood up and stepped near the water's edge, sure to keep a safe distance after what had just happened.

Was that how the girl fell in? Without anything blocking the edge, it would be easy to slip and fall. Her falling in could also have been mistaken for someone pushing her because of the huge crowd here for the festival. If that were the case, perhaps no one would have noticed when it happened.

Looking up at the sky, she noticed how dark it was getting. It seemed as if they had only left the house a little while ago. Clearly, it had been some time, judging by the sun setting over the river. It *was* pretty to look at, but it would have been better if her brother hadn't almost drowned in it.

"Alright, I think we should head home now."

Evan stood up. "I agree."

Following her brother as he tried to remember the way back to the house, she looked around. It was almost odd that no one was here by the river. *Had the story about the little girl scared them off? Or was something else going on?*

Brooke pondered these things in her head for a little while before noticing that Evan was limping. But it wasn't just that...

Feeling worried, she called to him, "Hey Evan, are you okay?"

Without looking back at her, he replied, "Yeah, why are you asking?"

After a moment, with no response, Evan stopped and looked over his shoulder. "What?" he asked again, this time looking a little concerned.

Brooke pointed down at his leg. It took a moment for him to realize what she was pointing at, but it quickly became clear. He twisted around to look behind him. Brooke watched as her brother looked down at his leg with a face of shock and horror. His pant leg was blood-stained and had a fairly large tear going down his calf.

Evan yelled, "My leg!"

A few people turned to see what all the commotion was about. Evan moved as swiftly as he could to the nearest bench and took a seat. Pulling his pants leg up, he could see a long gash on the back of his leg, going from just below the back of his knee to just above his ankle. Luckily, it wasn't still bleeding badly.

"I think you may have gotten cut or scraped by the rocks when you were scrambling not to fall in," said Brooke, examining his leg.

Their mother was a doctor, and when Brooke was younger, she always loved to listen to her mom explain the different ways to help people and what to do. Now, using this knowledge, she tried to figure out what she could do to help Evan. They didn't have a first aid kit, and that could be a problem.

"You should go wash it off and then put a cloth or something around it," she finally concluded, looking up at her brother.

"I am *not* going back to that river," he said, looking at her seriously.

"Obviously. Didn't you bring a water bottle with you?" Brooke replied, a little frustrated now.

"No. I thought *you* would bring it."

"Why would I bring *your* water bottle?" Brooke asked sarcastically.

"I don't know." Evan stopped talking long enough for them to think about what to do.

"You can still walk, right? I mean, you walked over here."

Brooke stood up and waited for a response. Evan stood up, looking a little worried, and then sat back down.

"Now that I know it looks like that, I don't want to make it worse," he said.

Brooke rolled her eyes. Sometimes, her brother could be the biggest baby in the world. Although she understood his concern, he couldn't just sit there on that bench all night. The day was almost over, and soon, the sky would be completely dark. Besides, if they already had trouble finding the house in daylight, it would be close to impossible in the dark. Plus, with her brother's wounded leg, she didn't know what to do.

Chapter 7

An Officer's Inquiry

Evan

A FTER EXAMINING HIS LEG, Evan noticed that Brooke was still standing there waiting for him to get up so they could head back to the house.

"Come on, it'll be dark by the time we get there," Brooke argued, trying to convince her brother to start moving.

Evan looked up at the sky and saw that she was right. The sun had almost completely set, and it was starting to get dark. After deciding he didn't want to try to find his way back to the house in the dark, he stood up. Walking toward Brooke, he looked back down at his leg. It didn't hurt much to walk, but he was sure that walking wasn't helping the wound.

"Finally," his sister said as he reached her.

"Let's just hurry and go home," he replied.

They began walking toward the festival exit. With Brooke following behind him, Evan headed down the sidewalk and tried to look for landmarks.

After walking a while, he noticed a poster taped to a tree and figured it was the same one they had passed earlier. Continuing, they passed a few other memorable landmarks and finally crossed the street to where the house was located. As they approached the driveway, Evan suddenly had a thought.

"So, what are we gonna tell Dad about my leg?"

Brooke paused, thinking it through. "I don't know; just tell him you were walking too close to the river when we went to check out the festival."

"You don't wanna tell him about the mystery, do you?"

Brooke waited a moment to respond. "Not yet. I need to make sure that it *is* a mystery first. Even though I'm quite sure, I could still be wrong."

Evan nodded, and they continued to the house. Going up the porch steps, they noticed their dad's car in the driveway. Evan shrugged as he went up to the door and knocked.

"Guess he got home before us."

A moment later, their father came and unlocked the door. "There you two are! I was wondering where you went."

He moved out of the way so they could enter the house. He closed the door behind them and continued, "So, did you have fun exploring today?"

Evan and Brooke looked at each other, and then Brooke replied, "Yeah, we went to check out the festival."

"I was going to go look around after my meeting, but I figured you kids were waiting for dinner, so I just came straight here instead."

He gestured toward the table. "Speaking of food, I hope you guys are hungry. I bought hamburgers and French fries for dinner."

Brooke glanced at Evan, wondering if he would talk. Once he didn't say anything, she began speaking.

"While we were checking out the festival, we ended up taking a path by the river. When we were walking by, Evan almost fell in, and he scraped his leg."

Their dad looked from her to Evan. "You shouldn't have gone by the river," he said. "Where did you get hurt?"

Evan reluctantly turned around and pulled his pant leg up to reveal the injury. After looking shocked for a moment, their father said, "You should see a doctor first thing tomorrow. Does it still hurt?"

"Not much. It looks worse than it feels." He pulled his pant leg back down.

"Good, alright. It doesn't look too deep, but I'll get a recommendation for a doctor and schedule an appointment for you tomorrow. Meanwhile, you two go eat your dinner."

As their father went upstairs to make the call, Brooke and Evan sat down at the kitchen table. After eating dinner, they both got up and went into the living room. Their dad had just returned from calling a doctor, and he went into the kitchen to eat. Turning on the TV, Evan flipped through a few channels to find something interesting to watch.

A knock on the door startled them. Brooke got up to answer it. She opened the door and was greeted by a security officer who introduced himself as Officer Wayne.

"Are you the Alans?"

Brooke answered, "Yes. Is there something you need?"

Officer Wayne nodded and told her about how he had seen two teenagers by the river near the festival. He had seen one teen almost fall in, but as he went to approach them with another officer, they had already left. Later, he discovered they were the children of Mr. Alans, the governor, who had been at the business meeting earlier today. Since he was on the mayor's security staff, he came to check on them to see if everything was alright.

"Neither of you are hurt, are you?"

Evan, who had joined his sister at the door, glanced at Brooke before he responded. "No, we're all right. Thank you for checking, though."

The officer gave a brief nod and was about to leave just as their father came to the door, wondering what was going on.

He greeted the guard as he walked to the door. "Hello, Officer. Is anything the matter?"

Shaking his head, Officer Wayne replied, "No, Sir, I just came to check on these two because of the incident at the river."

After a "thank you" from Mr. Alans and a curt "goodbye," Officer Wayne left. Their father went back into the kitchen to clean up and left them to themselves in the foyer.

Just then, Evan noticed Brooke staring at him. "What?"

She pointed to his leg and said, "You didn't tell the security officer about how you scraped your leg. You only said no one was hurt."

"So?" Evan replied defensively. "It's fine if I don't want people to know my business."

"Well, alright," Brooke said with a shrug and walked back into the living room.

It was true what he had said to his sister about it being his business, but he also didn't really trust the officer. With he and Brooke trying to solve the mystery, he thought it best to tell no one until it was solved. If he had told Officer Wayne about his injury, then he would have been questioned a little more, and eventually, the officer would get around to asking why they were there at the river in the first place.

Trying to put his thoughts aside, Evan walked past the living room and into his room. Sitting down on the bed, he thought over a few things. Tomorrow, because of his doctor's appointment, he wouldn't be able to go with Brooke to investigate—at least for a little while, anyway. Now that someone had found them near the river, it worried him that someone might also suspect that they were trying to figure out what really happened to that girl in the newspaper.

He started to think that maybe he was just being paranoid. That officer could have just been trying to help. He figured many people often stop by the river for the view, anyway. The sunset was beautiful, he remembered.

Now that he thought about it, he couldn't recall many details about the river, mainly because it wasn't a very memorable place. Ever since Evan could remember, he always had one mindset about things, depending on the situation, and it was difficult to change his mind. Now, because of what had happened at the river, he could only think of *that* place as somewhere to avoid.

Shrugging off his thoughts, he went to his suitcase to find something to wear to bed. After getting into his pajamas, Evan laid down in bed. It had been such a long day; he was feeling exhausted.

He closed his eyes and tried to fall asleep but realized he couldn't. After laying there for what seemed like forever, he finally drifted off. Despite everything that had happened, he was still excited to continue working on the case tomorrow.

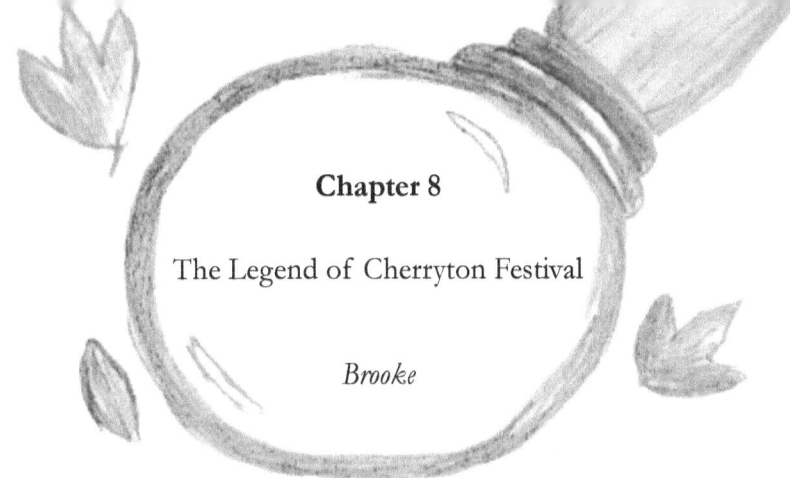

Chapter 8

The Legend of Cherryton Festival

Brooke

"SO, WHAT DID HE SAY?" Brooke asked her brother as he came back into the waiting room. Since Dad had a business meeting that day, Brooke went with her brother to the doctor instead.

"He said it'll be fine, but I should try to limit walking, so I don't hurt it more."

"Alright, then. Ready to go?" Brooke stood, and they left the doctor's office.

After walking a while, Brooke spoke. "Wanna head to the festival and see if we can figure out anything about the mystery?"

Evan was silent for a moment before responding. "Actually, I was gonna suggest going to the mayor's office. Once Dad's meeting ends, we could talk to the mayor and see if he has any information about the case."

"Alright, and I meant to tell you that while you were with the doctor, I overheard someone talking on their phone in the waiting room. They were saying something about how what happened in the newspaper sounded similar to something they'd heard before. I didn't really get to hear all that they were saying, but that sounds like a clue, doesn't it?"

Evan said, "Yeah, but they could've been talking about a different thing that happened in the newspaper. It's been a couple of days since the one with the article about the girl jumping into the river came out."

Well, that might be true, thought Brooke. But there's always a chance that it could have been what that lady was talking about. After a few more moments of thinking, she spoke.

"Alright, let's go to the mayor's office. He might know something about what I overheard, and it might be a clue. Even if he doesn't know anything, our visit won't be pointless. We were supposed to meet Dad after his meeting, anyway."

"Sounds good," answered Evan. "But next time, let's remember to bring our bikes. There's a lot of walking to do around New York," he said, glad he had made sure Dad brought their bikes along. "We could stop by the house and pick them up if you want," he suggested. "It's on the way."

"Alright, it *would* be quicker to get to the mayor's office that way," Brooke agreed.

* * * * *

Heading down the sidewalk, Brooke and Evan stepped onto the walkway leading to the main entrance of the mayor's office. After locking up their bikes, they went into the building. Walking up to the receptionist at the counter, they asked to see the mayor.

The receptionist looked up from her computer and smiled at them. "What do you two need to see the mayor for?"

"Our dad was in a meeting with him. He should be finished soon," Evan answered.

"Alright, I'll call his office."

They waited at the counter while the mayor was called. Once the receptionist set down the phone, she turned back to them.

"What's your last name?"

"Alans," Brooke responded.

"Okay, the mayor just finished his meeting with your father, so you two can go to his office. I'll show you where it is."

They followed the receptionist down the hall, up a flight of stairs, and then into an office. After being led inside, the door was closed behind them, and the receptionist left.

"What are you kids doing here?" asked their dad, turning around in his chair to look at them questioningly.

Brooke responded, "We wanted to talk to the mayor." She directed her attention to the other man sitting across the table from her dad, whom she assumed was the mayor.

"Once you're finished with your meeting," Evan quickly added.

The mayor turned his attention toward them and said, "Lucky for you two, the meeting just ended. But now I'm curious. What was it that you wanted to talk to me about?"

"Well, Mr. Mayor, we wanted to talk to you about the newspaper article… the one about the girl who jumped into the river," Brooke replied as the mayor gestured for them to take a seat.

"Please, call me Mayor Andrews, and yes, I remember that story—kind of odd for it to happen in the festival area. Not much happens there, you know. Anyway, is there any particular reason that you two would happen to be interested in it?"

"Actually, there is. We think something else may have happened, and the girl could have been pushed rather than jumped in. If I'm right with my geography, I'm almost certain that the Bloomington River hits a piece of land before going into the ocean. So, it would seem like the body would have already been found. Yet it's been days since the article was published, and no one has seen her," Brooke explained, hoping that Mayor Andrews would have some information, and this wouldn't be a dead end.

Mayor Andrews's expression changed to curiosity. "Oh, so I see... you're thinking of it as a mystery."

"Exactly," Brooke replied happily. "So, I was wondering if you had any information about it."

The mayor got up from his seat and began organizing his papers. "In that case," he said, "you consider yourself a detective solving a mystery, I suppose. Well, I don't have much to tell you about the newspaper article other than it being just another story in the paper. But since you seem like the kind that would believe in legends, I could tell you a story relating to the river."

Once Mayor Andrews finished speaking, he took a seat. Then, looking from Evan to Brooke, he waited for their response. After a quick nod from Brooke, he spoke again.

"Well, it's practically a tradition to tell it every year about this time, but you're not from around here, so I'll tell it to you now." After a pause, Mayor Andrews began the story.

"A long while ago, before this town was much of anything, there was a family that lived here named the Cherrytons. Mr. Cherryton was one of the first few mayors here, and his family was the main reason for the tradition of having the Cherryton Festival each year, although that's *not* why it's named after him. You see, the family was wealthy but kind and always ready to help people, although their children were very spoiled.

Unfortunately, the Cherrytons went bankrupt and lost much of what they had. They even ended up losing their house and had to move. After the bankruptcy, their children threw fits and temper tantrums, not wanting to move. A few days before they were scheduled to leave their home, their youngest daughter, who was nine years old, decided to cause a scene because she was upset about the move.

While her parents and siblings were outside, she went to the river and purposely jumped in. It's said that her goal was to scare her parents into thinking she drowned, and then she would swim upstream and wait for them to get back to the house. However, the current happened to be particularly strong that day, and it ended up pulling her under and carrying her away."

He paused, letting them take in the sad ending to the story before continuing. "It's believed that this story is the reason the Cherryton Festival is held so close to the river. Anyway, aside from that, later, once the Cherrytons passed away, a few of the people in town remembered their kindness and set up the tradition of the Cherryton Festival. It happens here every year now."

Once he finished with his story, Mayor Andrews looked back up at his listeners and smiled. "I don't know if that will help you much with your mystery, but it is an interesting legend that most of the people around here know."

Mr. Alans stood up and spoke, "Thank you for your time, Mayor, but we should get going. We don't want to keep you away from your work." He extended his hand.

Mayor Andrews stood up, shook his hand, and replied, "Yes, well, it was nice talking to you. I'll have those papers ready by tomorrow. I just need to call Mrs. Jones."

"I enjoyed speaking with you as well. Take your time with those papers. I won't need them until Thursday."

As Brooke, Evan, and their father walked to the door, Mayor Andrews called out, "I enjoyed speaking with you too, young lady, and good luck solving your mystery!"

After they closed the door behind them, they proceeded toward the lobby.

Turning to Evan, Brooke spoke quietly so only he could hear, "Doesn't it seem like an odd coincidence that the legend sounded a lot like the newspaper article?"

Evan whispered back, "I was thinking about that too. It almost seems like someone was trying to copy it."

"I knew it!" Brooke blurted out.

Thinking quickly, Evan said, "Um, knew what?"

"Uh... I knew it was more than a newspaper article. We've found our first clue, so that makes it an actual mystery!" Brooke explained happily as they entered the lobby.

Passing by the last office, Brooke could hear people talking rather loudly. Backing up to listen for a second, she tried to peek through the door.

"So, did you two just get back from investigating the river area?" The voice sounded young. Brooke figured it could be a teenage girl, probably about her age.

There were two other voices that sounded like older men. Brooke assumed they were guards or security officers, judging by the conversation, plus they were in the town hall.

"Yes, we just got back," one man said. "We couldn't find anything useful or related to the girl, though. We searched on both sides of the bank this time, too, and like Peter said, we didn't find anything."

The girl spoke again. "That's alright. Well, you two can go now. Since no one's been able to find anything around the river, you can stop searching."

"Right, so where should we look now?" asked the other man.

"Oh, I think you misunderstood me," the girl said. "I was suggesting we stop searching in general. It's pretty safe to say the girl's been washed all the way downstream by now."

The first man said, "That might be true, but shouldn't we still look? I mean… if there's a chance that she's still out there?"

"Listen, it's been days," the girl replied. "There's no way she could still be out there and alive. I say we call off the search. Besides, we've started to make a commotion down by the river. There have been too many officers sent down there lately, which has led people to wonder what's going on. I don't want anyone else to fall into the river. I'm sure you understand."

"Yes, Miss Andrews, we do," replied one of the men. Then Brooke could hear footsteps coming toward the door.

Turning to follow her father and Evan, she hurried out of the lobby. Glancing over her shoulder, she could see that she had moved away just in time as two security officers left the room and went out a back door. Behind them, a girl also exited, but she headed upstairs. She was about sixteen, Brooke guessed, a year older than her.

As Brooke joined him, Evan tapped her on the shoulder. "So, what was that all about? Now you're listening to private conversations?"

She looked at Evan and answered, "Just that one. They were talking about the river, so it was important for me to listen."

"Who's *they*?" asked Evan.

"Miss Andrews and two officers, I think."

He paused for a second, then spoke again. "*Miss Andrews?*" Confused, he asked, "Is that his wife… or *was* that his wife?"

"No," Brooke said. "She was too young. I think she's his daughter."

"Oh, yeah. I guess that makes sense," said Evan.

"Alright, kids, let's get your bikes in the car, and we'll head to the house," their dad said as he unlocked the car.

"Actually, I think I'll bike there if that's okay with you, Dad," Brooke said. "I want to check something out first."

Loading Evan's bike into the car, Brooke's dad called over his shoulder, "That's fine with me. Just be sure to get back before it gets dark. Alright?"

"Alright!" called Brooke. She waved as her dad drove off with Evan.

Brooke recalled everything she had just learned from the conversation she had heard. There were certainly a few things to think about—like what Miss Andrews had said about the river and not wanting people or officers to go near there. She also thought about the story the mayor had told her and how the newspaper article seemed to copy it closely.

As she walked her bike through the parking lot, she got lost in thought and didn't pay attention to where she was going. Brooke ended up bumping into someone who would play a big part in her mystery.

Chapter 9

Two New Suspects

Brooke

"OH, SORRY!" Brooke stood up and helped the other girl to her feet. "I guess I wasn't paying attention."

Dusting herself off, the girl replied, "You're fine, but next time you should watch where you're going."

Suddenly, the girl stopped and looked Brooke up and down.

"I don't think I've seen you before, and trust me, I know everybody around here. You're new here, aren't you?"

Nodding, Brooke replied, "Yeah, we're just visiting for a while."

After an awkward silence, the girl pulled out her phone and started swiping through the screens.

"My name's Brooke, by the way."

The girl looked up from her phone and replied, "My name's Whitney. Whitney Blaire." Continuing to scroll on her phone, she said, "I'm sure you've heard about me. I'm only *the* most popular person around here. In fact, my dad owns half of the businesses in this area."

Brooke didn't know who the girl was, but she nodded anyway. She opened her mouth to respond, but Whitney kept talking.

"My mother is the designer of a very popular clothing line as well. She owns boutiques in multiple states. Honestly, we should go shopping for some new clothes for you because those aren't really your style, Hon. No offense or anything."

Looking up from her phone once more to make sure Brooke was still listening, she asked, "So, what are you doing in New York? You said you were visiting, right?"

Brooke waited for a moment to make sure Whitney had really finished talking this time. "I'm here to try to solve a mystery."

Whitney stopped scrolling and asked, "The one about the girl and the river?"

Brooke replied. "Yep, good guess."

Whitney's expression immediately changed, and she glared at Brooke. "Well, you can stop your investigation because there's already a *real* detective on the case."

Brooke looked confused and questioned Whitney, "Who?"

Whitney looked straight at her and said, "*Me*, of course!"

"Really? Okay, well, we could maybe work together on it then. Two minds are better than one."

"No! One mind is better than two, and *that* mind is mine," Whitney responded sharply, pushing Brooke out of the way.

"What?" Brooke exclaimed. "Did you even know about the case before I told you about it?"

"No, but I'm the best at everything, so it shouldn't be hard for me to solve it before *you*."

Brooke just stared at her. They had only been talking for a few short minutes, and this girl had already gone from nice to just rude!

Whitney had begun walking off, but she stopped abruptly and turned around. "I know… why don't we make this a competition? Let's see who solves the case first."

"*You* can," Brooke said, "but I think I'll just try to solve it normally." Looking at her watch, she spoke again. "I need to go now. I've got to be home soon."

"Alright, bye. Don't expect to solve the mystery, though," Whitney said. "By the time you do, I'll have already solved it."

Brooke ignored her and began walking her bike again. Rolling her eyes, she was now even more determined to solve the case. She got on her bike and rode back to the festival, hoping to find more information about what happened.

* * * * *

Once she arrived at the festival, Brooke strolled around leisurely. It didn't look like anything had happened just a few days ago, and nothing really stuck out at first. She hadn't noticed anything in particular on her way to the river—that was until she got there. A quick glance revealed that it seemed the incident at the river *had* attracted more people to the festival. As Brooke approached the river, she saw quite a few people; there was even a group of kids playing with a frisbee. "*I guess once they heard about what happened, it led them to check out the festival. Interesting.*"

After searching around for a while and not finding anything that grabbed her attention, she decided it would be best to try talking to people. She noticed a woman sitting on a bench reading a newspaper. Walking up to her, Brooke said, "Hello."

Glancing up from her newspaper, the woman noticed Brooke. "Oh, hello," she said, smiling.

"Have you ever been to this festival before?" Brooke asked. "This is my first time around here."

"Actually, no, I haven't. I'm visiting and heard about what happened at the river, so I decided to come to the festival. I've enjoyed it so far. I even went down to check out the river, but I didn't see anything." The woman continued browsing through her newspaper as if trying to end the conversation.

Noticing this, Brooke replied, "Alright, well, it was nice talking with you."

She gave Brooke another glance and replied, "Nice talking with you, too."

Brooke turned and headed down the path, hoping for other people to question. As she was walking, she noticed something shining on the ground. She bent down and picked up the object to see what it was. It was an earring. Looking ahead, she saw a girl walking down the path in front of her.

Brooke ran to catch up with the girl and tapped her on the shoulder. "Um, excuse me. Did you drop this?" she asked as she held up the hand with the earring in it.

As the girl turned around, Brooke recognized her right away. She was the girl who had spoken with the two security officers at the town hall!

The girl felt her ear and then reached for the earring. She answered Brooke happily, "Yes, I did! I guess it must have fallen off. Thank you for picking it up."

She slid the earring into her pocket and then held out her hand. "I'm Kate, by the way."

Shaking her hand, Brooke responded, "My name's Brooke. Nice to meet you."

"Have you ever been to this festival before?" Kate asked, gesturing around.

"No, this is my first time. It happens every year, right?"

Kate replied, "Yeah. Every year, my dad, the mayor, puts together this festival. This year, it's special because I got to help with the planning."

"Cool! Well, it does seem like a lot of people have shown up for the festival, so it looks like you did good," Brooke replied.

"Thanks. You know, it's too bad that girl fell into the river. Everyone seems to think she was pushed, even though she wasn't," Kate said as she pulled out her phone. After scrolling for a second, she looked back up at Brooke. "Sorry, I just got a text from my mom. I've got to head home soon because we're having company come over."

"No problem," Brooke replied. She glanced at her watch; it read six o'clock. "I need to get home soon, too. I just came to check out the festival really quick."

"Alright. Well, that works out for both of us, I guess," Kate joked.

"Bye," Brooke said, starting toward her bike.

"Bye!" Kate called after her.

Brooke suddenly thought of something. She had checked the area where the river was, near the festival, but she hadn't checked across the river, on the other side. With this thought in her head, she got on her bike and rode to the opposite side.

Chapter 10

A New Ally

Brooke

A S BROOKE PEDALED to the other side of the river, she thought about her brief conversation with Kate. Now that she knew Kate was the mayor's daughter, it made a little more sense. Still, not all pieces of the puzzle were coming together just yet. Parking her bike by the water and walking to the river's edge, she observed a few things. First off, there was a railing here so no one could fall in, although on closer examination, it looked fairly new, and she wondered if it had been put there shortly after the incident.

Standing on this side of the river, she could clearly make out the other side. The river wasn't very wide, and you could probably throw a rock easily from one bank to the other. Looking away from the river, she spotted a fisherman sitting on a nearby bench, putting more bait on his line.

Brooke figured she could question him as well and see if she could find out anything else about the case. Before she could speak to him, the man greeted her first.

"'ello!"

"Hello!" Brooke called back, stopping near the bench. "Have you caught anything yet?" she asked, trying to start a conversation.

After slinging the line back into the water, he responded, "Not yet, I 'aven't. But it does look like it's gonna rain, so that might be why."

"Do you fish here often?"

"Sure do! As a matter of fact, I live right around 'ere. Come round every once in a while to fish in this 'ere river."

After a moment of silence, Brooke spoke up. "I was wondering, since you fish here often, did you happen to see the girl who fell in the river?"

Still focused on his line bobbing in the water, the man responded, "I can't say that I did."

After a moment of reeling the fishing line in and sighing, he tossed it back out. "Strange thing it was, one o' my buddies saw 'er the ot'er day, and 'e said she just jumped right in. With the current being fairly strong and all, she was immediately swept down with the flow of the river. Prutty strange, I'll say."

Just moments after the fisherman answered, another voice spoke up.

"Why do you ask? Are you trying to figure out what happened to her? So far, even the police don't know, or at least that's what they tell us."

Surprised, Brooke turned to see who was speaking. She realized it was a boy, probably about her age, sitting on the bench next to the fisherman. He and the boy both looked alike, so she assumed the fisherman was his father. The boy had been quiet the whole time they were talking, so she hadn't noticed he was there.

She said, "Yep, although *I* tend to think of it as a mystery that I'm trying to solve. It's proven to be interesting so far."

"Sounds cool," the boy said. "Do you need any help? I read a lot of mystery novels, and there's always someone who works with the detective." He handed the fisherman a box, and he reached inside and pulled out more bait.

"There's already someone trying to figure out the mystery with me. But you can help if you want! The more people, the sooner it'll get solved," Brooke replied with a smile.

"Alright, cool. So, what do we know so far?" asked the boy. "Oh, and my name's Thomas, by the way."

"My name's Brooke, and this might take a while." Then Brooke began telling him about what she had learned so far in the case. She finished up by telling him about how she found the earring and talked with the mayor's daughter.

After she finished, Thomas spoke. "Well, that *does* seem a little weird. That whole thing about the mayor's daughter, I mean, it's almost like she doesn't want officers near the river for a reason."

"True, but if we want to solve this, we're gonna need a lot more information to go on," Brooke replied.

Suddenly, an idea popped into her head. She rushed to the newspaper stand, grabbed a newspaper, and began scanning articles until she found the one she was looking for.

"Here!" she said, pointing at a paragraph.

Looking to where her finger was pointing, Thomas read aloud,

> Local officials investigated the area around the river once more, and, finding no sign of Julie, claimed her to be dead. Nine-year-old Julie Rosette Peters died on November 17th at 4:37

p.m., as a result of falling into the river when the current was particularly strong. She will be missed by all her friends and loved ones, especially her mother and father, Sylvia and Kevin Peters. For the past nine years, the family has lived on Elmwood Avenue. A spokesperson for the family reports that since the death of their daughter, the parents are considering moving back to their hometown, south of New York. Julie's funeral procession will take place on November 25th in Port View Park's Cemetery.

Once he had finished reading, he said, "So, they think she's dead."

Nodding, Brooke replied, "Yes, but they haven't found her body, so they don't know for certain. Remember, I heard Kate telling them not to check the river again. That means we don't even know when the last time they looked was. But that wasn't what I was talking about. Notice anything else?"

Thomas scanned the paragraph again. "Um, no. What am I looking for?"

"Clues that will help us figure out something about the mystery," she replied, handing him the newspaper. "See anything like that?"

After examining it once more, Thomas handed the paper back to her. "Well, they'll be having the funeral in Port View Park Cemetery. I don't think that's really a clue, though."

"Look," Brooke said, pointing and reading aloud. "She will be missed by all her friends and loved ones, especially her mother and father, Sylvia and Kevin Peters. The family lived for nine years on Elmwood Avenue." After checking to see if

Thomas was catching on, she continued. "It says where Julie lived, so we should question the people on Elmwood Avenue to see if they knew anything about Julie."

"Oh, that makes sense. They'll probably know why she went down to the river in the first place, and at least we'll get some information about her," Thomas concluded.

"Exactly." Brooke was glad she didn't have to continue trying to explain it. Glancing down at her watch, she hurried to her bike. "Sorry, I have to get going. I was supposed to be back at the house a little while ago."

After placing the newspaper in her bag, she got on her bike. "We can meet up tomorrow at Elmwood Avenue and question people there around noon."

"Alright, see you then," called Thomas as Brooke rode off down the sidewalk.

She tried to hurry as she pedaled toward the house. She was supposed to be back before it got dark, and now the sun had almost finished setting. Brooke figured that if she pedaled fast enough, she'd get there right before the sun officially went down. Lucky for her, she was right.

Turning the street corner, she rode up and parked her bike in the garage before heading inside. As she entered, she noticed her dad with papers sprawled across the table, looking up at her.

"When I said for you to get home before dark, I didn't think you would get home exactly a second before the sun went down."

"Sorry, Dad."

"Well, did you find out anything else about your mystery?"

"Actually, I figured out a lot more." Brooke told him about Kate and how she figured out she was the mayor's daughter. She concluded with how Thomas offered to help with the mystery.

"Cool. Sounds like you've got it all figured out," he responded as he scribbled something down on a piece of paper. "I have a little more work to catch up on, but I'll have the table cleared off in time for dinner."

Brooke nodded, then left the kitchen. As she did, her father called, "I'm gonna order a pizza. You like cheese, right?"

"Yep!" she called happily from the other room.

Brooke went up the stairs and into the room she was staying in. She sat down on the bed. Picking up the remote, she switched on the TV, trying to find something to do, when someone knocked on her door.

"You can come in," she called, assuming it was her brother.

The door opened, and Evan started talking. "Have you read today's newspaper yet?"

Nodding, Brooke responded, "Yeah, a little while ago. Tomorrow, Thomas and I are going to head down to Elmwood Avenue, where Julie used to live, and question some people. Wanna come?"

"Sure, sounds interesting. Who's Thomas?" Evan asked, looking at the newspaper in his hand.

"A new friend I made who's gonna help with the mystery. His dad is a fisherman, and his friend witnessed her go into the river," she replied, setting down the remote. Then, Brooke paused for a second.

"What?" Evan asked, turning to his sister.

Brooke hesitated before speaking. "Yeah. The fisherman's friend actually said she *jumped* in. You know, it seems a little odd that Kate was so sure the girl fell in and wasn't pushed."

"And now this guy says she jumped in," Evan said thoughtfully.

Brooke sighed and said, "Right."

Chapter 11

Brietta's Boutique and Tailor Shop

Thomas

A FTER GETTING DRESSED, Thomas went downstairs to breakfast. "Come on, or your eggs will get cold!" teased his dad as Thomas entered the kitchen. After taking a seat, he checked his watch. It read 8:18. At twelve, he was supposed to meet up with Brooke to work on the case.

"Got somethin' on your mind?" asked his father. He sat down across from Thomas. "You look like you're thinkin' 'bout somethin' interestin.'"

After looking up from his watch and eating a bite of egg, Thomas responded. "I guess I'm just excited about solving an actual mystery." Looking over, he saw his father smile.

"Oh yeah, you and that Brooke girl were gonna try to figure out what 'appened to that girl who fell in the river. You always loved mysteries."

"Yeah, and it's cooler now that I get to try to solve one," Thomas added before taking another bite of egg and toast.

His father took a bite of his own breakfast and then spoke again. "I plan on tryin' to fish at the river again today. I got me some new bait that I think will work this time." After a quick pause to look up and see if his son was still listening, he continued. "Maybe you might wanna come fishin' with me again after you finish your mystery thing?"

"Sounds like fun," Thomas replied, smiling at his dad. "Just as long as Big Bob doesn't come around again." Thomas's dad looked up and smiled at him. "We'll just 'ave to be careful."

Big Bob was a joke that Thomas and his father loved to repeat ever since "Big Bob" showed up. Thomas chuckled to himself every time he thought about it. It all started when, one day, he and his dad were fishing by the river. His dad was making jokes that weren't very funny, and he was playing along and laughing when they saw a huge shadow in the water.

Convinced he might catch it as soon as it got the bait, Thomas's dad tried to reel it in. The problem was that the fish was so enormous that it started to reel *him* in instead. Thomas's dad fell into the river and got pulled by the fish for a short way before giving up and letting go of the rod. Coming out of the water, soaking wet and laughing, he exclaimed, "I 'ope I never see that darned Big Bob again." That was exactly how the joke about Big Bob came to be.

He chuckled to himself, recalling the memory as he left the table to put his dish in the sink. Suddenly, another thought occurred to him. After looking around the room for a second, he asked, "Hey, Dad, have you seen Bear today?"

Bear was half Great Pyrenees, half Anatolian Shepherd, and *all* energy. Usually, he came bounding into the kitchen the second he smelled breakfast. *This* morning, though, Thomas hadn't seen him yet.

After taking a sip of his tea, his father smiled. "Oh, Bear? I could 'ave sworn I told you, but I guess not. I dropped 'im off at the vet early this morning before you were up. It's time for 'is annual check-up, you know."

Oh yeah, that's right, he thought to himself. It was a little odd without Bear around the house, but Thomas knew Bear would be back where he belonged by the time he returned home.

Thomas glanced down at his watch and noticed that it read 9:10. Seeing the time brought his mind back to the mystery. *Okay, so I've got a few hours before I have to meet up with Brooke.* Usually, at this time of day, a kid would be in school, but since Thomas was home-schooled, as long as he finished his schoolwork for the day, he could do his assignments anytime.

Upstairs in his room, he sat down at his desk and pulled out his binder. His first subject was math, so he took out the worksheet and got to work on it. The time quickly flew, and before he knew it, the clock read 12:23.

He hurried downstairs to the garage, got on his bike, and rode speedily to Elmwood Avenue. Once he arrived, he parked his bike and then began looking around for Brooke.

It didn't take him long to find her. The street was fairly short and ended at a dead end. Halfway down, he noticed her talking to someone who appeared to be working as a painter.

Thomas walked over to them, reaching Brooke just as she finished talking. "Perfect timing. That lady had some information on Julie that I found pretty interesting," Brooke said excitedly.

"Cool, what'd you find out?" Thomas asked, eager to start solving the mystery.

"That was Mrs. Malley Wright, and she's clearly a painter from the looks of what she was wearing. But that's not the important information. The stuff I found out was this... Julie is well-known around here. In fact, she used to live here before the incident at the river. That lady told me that Julie was an actor, and she always loved being in the spotlight. She used to take dance and singing classes, and every year, she would put on a play with her parents for their neighbors and friends," Brooke told Thomas, finally stopping to take a breath.

"Interesting," replied Thomas.

"But that's not all," she continued. "Mrs. Wright also said she saw Julie at the tailor shop on the same day she fell into the river. She said Julie was looking at dresses, and she thinks she may have bought one that looked expensive."

Thomas asked, "So, did Mrs. Wright say what time Julie bought a dress?"

"Good question, but no, she didn't. Although we *do* know it was sometime before 4:37 p.m. because that's when she fell into the river." Brooke replied. "You know, it's actually kind of sad that she got a new dress and wasn't even able to wear it."

Suddenly, Thomas piped up, "Maybe she wore it to the festival, and she was wearing heels or something, and that caused her to fall in."

Brooke considered this for a second. "That's a good point, but who wears a fancy dress to a festival? If she were going to attend, it would have gotten dirty. Besides, if she planned to go on any rides, it might have gotten caught on something."

"True," he responded, "but it was just a guess."

After a moment of silence, Thomas spoke up again. "Why don't we head to the place where she bought her dress? We could see if the owner has any information about Julie to give us."

"Alright, sounds good to me," Brooke replied, nodding as she got on her bike. Then, they set off toward the tailor shop.

* * * * *

They arrived at the boutique and got off their bikes. As they headed to the front of the shop, Thomas paused for a moment to look at the exterior of the building. It was made of bricks and painted a light gray, with plenty of windows showcasing dresses and designer clothes. Looking up at the sign glowing above their heads, he read it aloud.

"Brietta's Boutique and Tailor Shop. We fix your dresses and make them, too."

"Has a nice ring to it," Brooke said, stepping through the sliding glass double doors.

Thomas followed, and as he entered, he almost bumped into a saleswoman hurrying to bring an upset customer a dress.

As he looked around, the first thing he noticed was that the place was too bright. The few dozen chandeliers attached to the ceiling made the white tile floor and white walls almost glow. Aside from that, there were dresses on racks everywhere and a row of light gray floor tiles leading from the door to the counter.

As they walked to the front of the store, a lady wearing sunglasses stood behind the counter, looking down at them. She removed her sunglasses for a moment, typed something on her computer as if she were in a rush, and then hurried behind a curtain in the back.

"I can see why she needs to wear sunglasses," Brooke whispered jokingly into Thomas' ear. He cracked a smile and nodded as the lady with the sunglasses came back to the counter.

"Can I help you two with something?" she asked, sounding nicer than she looked.

"Yes," Brooke replied with a glance at the lady's name tag. "Brietta, we were wondering if you knew anything about Julie Peters."

Brietta's smile faded, and she looked quizzically at them for a moment. "Why are you wondering?"

Brooke smiled and responded calmly, ignoring Brietta's suspicious glare. "Someone told us that you made all the costumes for Julie's plays. We figured that since you saw her last, you might be able to tell us if you knew any information about her."

Looking back and forth between them, Brietta spoke, clearly annoyed. "Oh, so you both came here to spy on me. What, since I'm the last person who spoke to Julie, you're making me your number one suspect?"

Brooke quickly spoke, "What? No! We just wanted to speak with you a little bit about..."

But before she could finish, Brietta cut her off. "I heard you already. You want to know about Julie. I don't plan on telling you anything since you're blaming me for being the one who made her jump in the river. All I do is make her dresses," she said with a quick gesture around her. "Now leave!"

Brooke and Thomas both looked at each other for a moment, dumbfounded. Clearly, Brietta would not listen to them if she thought they were blaming her.

Thinking fast, Thomas spoke up. "Well, the main reason we came here wasn't to talk about Julie. It was to find out who made all her amazing costumes!" he said with a fake smile, glancing at Brooke.

Catching on to what he was doing, Brooke smiled at Brietta. "That's right! We're huge fans of theater, and some of Julie's dresses she used in her plays are fantastic!"

Brietta stopped and looked at them. "Well, I *do* design them all myself," she said rather snottily.

"I can tell. They all have that special touch!" Brooke said a little too enthusiastically.

Brietta still looked skeptical of them, but her annoyance seemed to have changed into pride—pride in herself, that is.

"Alright, you two, enough with the flattery. What do you kids want?"

Brooke cast a quick glance at Thomas as if to say, "Now, how do we ask her about Julie without her going bananas again?"

After a moment of consideration, Thomas responded to Brietta.

"Well, you see, my friend here loves to wear dresses, especially fancy designer ones. Anyway, her birthday's coming up, and she really liked that last dress you sold to Julie. She was wondering if you had any more like it."

Brietta looked clearly proud of herself and immediately began bragging. "Well, I make *all* my dresses unique. In fact, I don't think I've ever made two that are the same. If you really wanted it, I suppose I could make another one for you. I should warn you, though, it won't be the same; it'll be even better!"

Suddenly, the phone rang, and Brietta hurried to answer it. "One moment, please," she said.

After her call, she set the phone down and returned.

"You know, I made *all* the costumes Julie wore in *all* her plays. She's only ever ordered her dresses from *me*, as a matter of fact. That last dress I sold to her was my fanciest one yet! Do you want to know something? She told me she was going to wear it to a big event, and I told her that when she wears the new dress I made for her, *she'll* be the big event!"

Brietta went to the back curtain. "Give me just a second, and I'll be ready to write down your order."

After she disappeared behind the curtain, Brooke turned to Thomas. "That was genius! You convinced her to tell us exactly what we needed to know about Julie without her even knowing it."

Thomas smiled. "Thanks! But now we need to figure out a way for her not to freak out when we tell her you're not getting any dresses."

The curtain moved, indicating someone was about to come out from behind it.

Assuming it was Brietta, Brooke whispered, "Good luck."

Both chuckling at the joke, they turned back toward the curtain. Just as they did, indeed, someone came out from behind the curtain, but it was *not* Brietta.

Thomas noticed Brooke's expression change as the girl came toward them, looking down at her phone as she walked. He also noticed that she looked a lot like Brietta and wondered if they might be related.

Stopping behind the counter in front of them, the girl spoke, still facing her phone. "My mom's busy right now. She'll be with you in a second."

The door to the shop opened, and the girl looked up. After smiling at the person entering, she noticed Brooke.

Shocked, she asked, "What are *you* doing here?" She looked Brooke up and down.

Brooke replied, "What are *you* doing here…Whitney?"

Chapter 12

A Strange New Clue

Brooke

"WHAT DO YOU MEAN, what am *I* doing here? This is my mom's boutique. I told you she was a clothes designer, or did you already forget that?" Whitney glared at Brooke and rolled her eyes dramatically.

"Actually, I didn't, but there are literally a dozen boutiques in New York. How was I supposed to know this one was your mom's?" Brooke asked, with a clearly annoyed look on her face.

"Couldn't you tell?" snapped Whitney, gesturing around her.

"No," Brooke replied.

"Whatever!" Whitney said, annoyed. Rolling her eyes again, Whitney looked back down at her phone.

Confused, Thomas looked at Whitney and then back at Brooke before he spoke. "Um, am I missing something here?"

Whitney looked at him as if just noticing he was there. After staring for a moment, she turned back to Brooke, completely ignoring Thomas. "So, what are you doing here?"

"We came here to try to work on the mystery," Brooke replied.

Whitney wrinkled her nose at Brooke. "Well, *don't* bother. I already figured it out!" she said triumphantly. "It was really easy, you know... once I examined the clues and stuff." She sounded quite proud of herself.

Looking directly at Whitney, Brooke responded, "Really? Well, congratulations. So, what did you figure out happened to her?"

Whitney snapped, "I'm not going to tell you! *I* was the one who figured it out, so I deserve *my* name in the papers. So why don't you go run along and find something better to do?"

Just as Brooke opened her mouth to respond, Brietta came back through the curtain with a clipboard and pencil. "Alright, I'm back. Sorry for the long wait. I couldn't find my clipboard."

Whitney looked from her mom to Brooke, and then a smirk came on her face. "You're buying something?" she asked jokingly. "You *do* know these are designer dresses, right? Not just some ten-dollar thing you get at a thrift store."

Brietta gave a quick look toward Whitney just as the door opened and another customer walked in. "That must be Rose. She scheduled an appointment yesterday to try on some dresses." Turning to Whitney, Brietta said, "Why don't you go help her out?"

"Sure, Mom," she replied, walking to the curtain, clearly upset. As she left, Brooke saw her peek over her mother's shoulder at the clipboard. Then she eyed Brooke with a smirk on her face.

"You're getting *that* dress? Like you have that much money. Plus, girl, you could never pull that off."

Setting the clipboard down and turning to her daughter, Brietta said, "Whitney!"

Still glaring at Brooke, Whitney hurried to help Rose.

Brietta gave Thomas and Brooke a weak smile. "Sorry about my daughter. She can be a little... um... stubborn."

Laughing to himself, Thomas whispered, "A little?"

Brooke heard him and quietly chuckled as Brietta went over to type something on her computer.

Brietta said, "You know, as a matter of fact, Mr. and Mrs. Peters just came the other day to pick up her dress—Mrs. Peters' dress, that is." She continued speaking and retrieved her clipboard, "You know, it's actually a bit odd. They just walked in, picked up the dress, and then left. They didn't even say a word to me or any of my workers. Just picked it up and left."

She handed the clipboard to Brooke. "Alright, now, if you could just write down your name and how you'll be paying. Also, we don't do shipping. So, you'll need to come pick up your dress once it's done," she said, smiling broadly.

"Um, how much is the dress?" Brooke asked cautiously.

Brietta looked back across the counter. "Well, let me think. Let's see. I work hard on all my dresses, adding to each of them their own special touch, as you mentioned earlier. Plus, I take individual measurements of each person and try to tailor them to their unique style. Also, this is my most expensive dress, but it really is worth its price. Finally, she answered Brooke's question.

"So, how does one thousand five hundred dollars sound?"

Brookes' eyes widened when she heard the price. She looked back at Brietta and asked, "How about your other dresses? You've made a bunch of nice ones." Brooke was smiling at her with a smile that was clearly fake.

Brietta bought it, though, and went on telling Brooke about *all* her other dresses. The time flew, and before they knew it, Brietta had been talking for more than thirty minutes.

Looking down at her watch, Brooke spoke up. "It's almost six o'clock, and we've got somewhere to be. Maybe I can come back later and look at dresses, then?"

Brietta smiled. "Sure. Just remember, I make *all* my dresses special. This is the only boutique you'll find in New York that makes designer dresses like these. Have a nice day!"

"You too," Thomas said politely, and the two of them left the boutique. Once the door closed, he asked, "How long were we there?"

"We got here about five, so maybe about an hour."

"It felt longer than that," he said.

"True, but we learned some information about Julie," Brooke reminded him.

"A little odd that the Peters picked up a dress just a few days after their daughter supposedly died," Thomas said.

Brooke turned to him. "I was thinking the same thing. But maybe Mrs. Peters picked up a funeral dress."

Thomas looked like he didn't believe that, but he replied anyway, "Yeah, maybe."

After a few moments of walking, he suddenly spoke. "Wait, you said that it's around six, right?"

"Yeah, why?" Brooke questioned.

"I've gotta get back to my dad. I told him that I'd go fishing with him before it got dark," Thomas responded as he began rushing off.

"Alright. Let's meet up again at Elmwood Avenue tomorrow, around twelve again. Sound good?"

Thomas replied, "Sounds good!"

As Thomas left, Brooke got on her bike and began riding back to the house. As she rode, she thought over the things she had just learned, other than precisely how much it cost and how long it took to make every dress in the boutique.

She had discovered that Brietta made all of Julie's dresses for her plays and that Julie had bought a dress from Brietta not long before jumping or falling into the river. She had also learned that Julie's parents had purchased a dress almost the day after Julie's supposed death.

As Brooke was thinking things through, she was suddenly interrupted by a loud crash. Turning her bike around, she hurried over in the direction of the sound to see what happened. She got off her bike and saw there was a tipped-over trash can and a bike on the sidewalk. Brooke looked closer and saw that someone must have just fallen off their bike. She stepped closer and realized that it was...

"Thomas?" Brooke asked, confused. She rushed to help him up. "What happened?"

Standing up and brushing himself off, Thomas replied. "I was riding back to my house when some lady ran right past the front of my bike. I swerved to avoid hitting her and crashed right into that garbage can!" He motioned at the sideways trash can on the ground.

"Oh, is that all?" Brooke asked, helping pick up the trash can, which was luckily empty.

"Is that all?" Thomas repeated, slightly annoyed. "I'm glad I was wearing a helmet!" he added, picking his bike back up.

"Oh, yeah, sorry," Brooke replied. "I just wanted to know if it had anything to do with the case."

"Well, lucky for you, it did. At least, I think so." Thomas held onto his bike, so it didn't fall again. "The lady who ran in front of my bike said something kinda strange. She said, 'Watch out for the squirrel. It knows it's alive.'"

"What squirrel? What does that have to do with the mystery?" Brooke asked.

"I don't know," Thomas shrugged. "But it's scary to think that squirrels know anything at all. They're getting smarter."

Brooke rolled her eyes and laughed. "Are you sure she said squirrel and not something else that sounded similar?" Brooke asked.

"Well, that's a possibility. But in the meantime, we should start looking for squirrels. It's like bird watching. While we've been squirrel watching, sounds like the squirrels have been people watching!" Thomas joked.

"Um, I don't think so. What else could that lady have been saying? What rhymes with squirrel?" Brooke asked.

Thomas threw out some guesses. "Hmm, pearl. Or maybe twirl?"

Brooke continued thinking until Thomas suddenly blurted out, "I've got something!"

"You figured it out?" Brooke asked, hopefully.

"Kinda," Thomas continued with a grin. "When I was little, there was this old amusement park ride my dad would always take us on that spun around super-fast. It was a lot of fun, and you always felt sick afterward 'cause it went so fast."

Thomas turned to see Brooke staring at him blankly. "Okay…" Brooke waited a moment, and when Thomas didn't continue, she said, "Go on."

Thomas snapped back to reality. "Anyway, it was called 'The Hurl n' Whirl' 'cause that's pretty much what happened after you went on it. And since *squirrel* rhymes with both *hurl* and *whirl*…."

"Do you really think that's what the lady said?" Brooke asked.

"Well, squirrels are definitely up to something!"

"What?" Brooke asked, stifling a giggle. "What is it with you and squirrels?"

"Uh… never mind," Thomas replied sheepishly.

"Kay then…" Brooke said, chuckling as she went back to thinking about other possible words—ones that actually seemed more logical.

After considering things for a moment, Brooke said, "I know! I think a word that makes sense to switch for the first part is *girl* instead of *squirrel*. Besides, I'm almost positive it's not *hurl*."

"Yeah, that makes a lot more sense than my guess," Thomas laughed.

"But it doesn't make sense to say the girl knows she's alive. Of course, she knows that!" Brooke said.

"Hmm. What about another word for the second part?" Thomas suggested. "Like maybe the other word is something else instead of alive?"

"Sure, maybe. A tie? A fly? A try?" Brooke offered.

Thomas said, "I got nothing."

Brooke sighed and resumed thinking quietly.

After enduring a bit of silence, Thomas spoke up. "Wow. This is a lot harder than I thought. Whoever said detective work was easy sure told a lie."

"Yeah," Brooke agreed absentmindedly. Then her face lit up! "Wait! That's it!" she shouted.

"What? What?" Thomas asked, surprised by her outburst.

Brooke shook him by the shoulders. "It's a lie! It's a lie!"

Totally confused, Thomas cried, "What? What's a lie? What lie?"

Brooke took a deep breath, calmed herself, and spoke. "Don't you see? It's not she knows *she's alive*... she knows *it's a lie*!"

Thomas' expression changed as her words sunk in. "Wow. You did it! That's *got* to be it."

Excited by decoding what the woman said, Brooke repeated it aloud, "Watch out for the girl. She knows it's a lie."

Turning back to Thomas, she asked, "You know what that means, right?"

"Right. It means now we have to figure out who the girl is."

"Exactly! Any ideas?" Brooke asked.

"Not yet. But it's getting dark, and I better hurry and get going." Thomas climbed back onto his bike.

"You're right. We'll figure it out. See you tomorrow," Brooke called to him as he pedaled away.

Getting back onto her own bike, she thought about what the lady had said and what a great clue it was. "Watch out for the girl. She knows it's a lie."

Recalling the people she knew had something to do with the case, the first person who came to mind was Whitney.

After considering a few more people, she was rather stumped. Until…

"Wait, I think I've got it!" she announced to no one in particular. Now, Brooke was sure she had figured out who the person was. It was the only girl it could possibly be.

And by the way, who was that lady?

Chapter 13

The Footprints

Thomas

Q UICKSAND...THOMAS was sinking in quicksand, grasping to hold on to anything to pull himself up!

Suddenly, a woman walked up to him. Leaning forward, she whispered into his ear, "Watch out for the girl. She knows. It's a lie."

Then she ran off and vanished into the night. As the woman disappeared, Thomas groped about, desperately searching for something to pull himself out, but there was no use. His head was almost under the quicksand. He kept going lower and lower and lower. Until....

"Ahh!" He gasped and quickly sat up in his bed. A frantic search around the room confirmed that he wasn't sinking in quicksand but had just woken up from a nightmare.

Lying back down, Thomas couldn't seem to fall back asleep, no matter how hard he tried. Reluctantly, he got up and switched on the light, looking up at his clock on the wall. "5:20 a.m.," he read aloud. "I'll never be able to fall back asleep now."

He paced back and forth in his room, wondering what to do. He didn't want to wake up his father, who was sleeping down the hall. Although his dad tended to wake up early, he never woke up *this* early. He usually got up around 6:30.

Thomas sat down at his desk and decided to go through what he knew about the case. Getting out a piece of paper and a pencil, he wrote down a few of the main notes that were important to the mystery. He ended the list with a note about what the lady had said in his dream.

Now, the white clock ticking on the wall read 6:37. With surprise, he realized it had taken longer than he thought to scribble down his notes. Thomas set down his pencil and went downstairs just in time to see his dad come out of his room, stretch, and yawn.

* * * * *

Riding down the sidewalk on his bike, Thomas eventually arrived at Elmwood Avenue. As he parked his bike, he noticed Brooke standing near a bakery, talking with someone. Once she saw him, she waved him over.

"Hey Thomas, we're over here," Brooke called. When he reached them, Brooke introduced him to her brother.

"Thomas, this is my older brother Evan. He's helping with the mystery, too." Then, turning to Evan, she continued. "Evan, this is my new friend Thomas. He's been helping with the mystery while you were letting your leg heal."

The boys shook hands, and after a "nice to meet you" from each of them, Brooke spoke.

"Okay, so I just filled Evan in on the stuff we've learned so far."

"Yes, lots of details," Evan said.

"We're about to head to the mayor's office to go over what we know with Mayor Andrews," Brooke continued. "We haven't spoken to him since a few days ago, and now I think we have some key information."

"Sounds good to me," Thomas replied, and the three began walking down the sidewalk toward the mayor's office.

"Don't we need our bikes?" Evan asked, unsure as they began walking.

"We should be fine," Thomas replied. "It won't take that long to walk there from here."

After walking for a few minutes, Brooke asked Thomas, "Did I ever tell you that I figured out what the lady meant?"

"Um, what lady?" came Thomas's confused reply.

"The one who made you crash your bike."

After a moment of recalling his nightmare, he replied. "No, you didn't tell me."

"Alright. Well, remember how we figured out that she said, 'Watch out for the girl. She knows it's a lie?' Well, after you left yesterday, I tried to think of all the girls who have something to do with this case, and after a while, I figured out who she was talking about."

"You did?" asked Thomas.

"Yep. It's Kate," Brooke said triumphantly.

Thomas, who had a confused look on his face, asked, "Who's Kate?"

Evan, who had just been given a recap by Brooke a few minutes ago, spoke up. "Kate is the mayor's daughter. She was the one who set up the festival this year."

"Oh, alright. So, what does she have to do with the mystery?" Thomas asked.

"Clearly too much," Brooke replied. "She's the only one related to the case who is shy. Once I thought about it yesterday, she has a *lot* to do with the river as well."

"How?" both boys asked at the same time.

Brooke replied with a smile. "You'll figure it out soon. Now, let's go speak with the mayor."

They had arrived at the mayor's office quicker than Thomas thought they would. After stepping through the large glass double doors, he realized he had never been inside this building before. Sure, he had ridden by a couple of times on his bike, but he never had a reason to go inside… until now, that is.

As the trio walked in, Thomas noticed Brooke was heading straight to the receptionist's desk. Following, he and Evan stopped behind her and waited in line behind a few other people who were also wanting to speak with the receptionist. He saw that most of the objects in the lobby were white, along with white walls and a white tile floor. There was a chandelier above the central area, as well as above the front desk. To the left of the desk, he noticed a stairway going to the end of a hall and a few doors to the sides of it.

Thomas didn't usually notice or even pay attention to details. But with this place being so nicely decorated and fancy, it was hard not to notice the muddy footprint on one corner of the carpet where all the seats were located. Scanning the people around him, he wondered if one of them could have left it.

Turning and tapping Brooke on the shoulder, he pointed out the print on the rug. "Look, someone left a muddy footprint on the rug there."

Brooke saw the footprint. She turned to Evan. "Can you keep our place in line? I think Thomas found some evidence."

Before he could respond, she began walking to the supposed evidence, with Thomas following her. They both got on their knees and examined the footprint.

After a moment of consideration, Thomas said, "I'd say it looks like a high-heeled shoe print." He pointed. "Notice how it's kind of separated at the heel?"

Nodding, Brooke responded, "Well, that certainly makes it easy! Now we know it was a woman." She quickly scanned the room and then turned back to Thomas, disappointed.

"Whoever it was must have already left, though. All the women in here are wearing sneakers or boots."

"Also, the footprint is pointing toward the stairs. So, they must have gone that way," Thomas added.

Brooke looked toward the stairs and then back at the footprint.

"What I can't understand is why there's only *one* footprint. If the lady had muddy shoes, then there would be footprints from the door to here. But there's not. This is the only one."

"There's always a chance they mopped recently," Thomas said. "It's a lot harder to clean carpet, you know."

After a curious glance from Brooke, Thomas was quick to explain. "I have a dog."

As she continued examining the footprint, Thomas glanced from the door to the stairs. As he did, he noticed something. He moved closer to it and called back to Brooke, "Hey, look! I found another footprint!"

Brooke hurried over, her expression changing from excited to confused.

"Huh, this is a different footprint than the one on the carpet," she observed.

"Yeah. It looks like one from a tennis shoe. So, either there was more than one person with muddy shoes, or someone had a different shoe on each foot."

Brooke nodded in agreement as she continued studying the new footprint.

"Well, that means neither point really works now."

"Which points?" Thomas asked curiously.

"Well, first, they haven't mopped recently. If they had, this second print wouldn't be here because it's on the tile. With that being said, these are the only tracks. None coming from the door, none going up the stairs. It's like someone literally jumped through the window, landed here, then took their shoes off and just walked away." She shrugged, feeling confused.

"What's the second point?" Thomas asked.

"Well, I guess the second point is just an idea," she said. "But I'm guessing that it was one person wearing two different shoes. Notice how the shoe size is about the same?" Brooke pointed at both footprints.

"There's also something else you didn't mention," Thomas said after Brooke had finished speaking.

"What's that?"

"Well, you didn't say anything about the fact that there are two muddy footprints here, and it hasn't rained in days."

"Good point, Thomas! I was actually here a few days ago, and the footprint wasn't there. It hasn't rained since then!"

Thomas studied both footprints. "So, how did two muddy footprints get here?"

"You tell me," was Brooke's response.

An idea suddenly occurred to Thomas, and his face lit up. "Okay, I will! If it hasn't rained for days, and these two footprints just got here a while ago, then where did the mud come from?"

He watched Brooke to see if she was going to respond. Seeing she wasn't, he continued. "Well, we both know that a huge part of this mystery is the river. That's pretty much what this whole thing is about. Whoever it was must have been near the river to get mud on their shoes," Thomas finished triumphantly.

"Hey, good point!" Brooke said excitedly. "Well then, there are only two questions."

"What are they?" Thomas asked.

After glancing at each footprint again, she said, "The same two questions we were wondering earlier… how did these footprints get here, and who left them?"

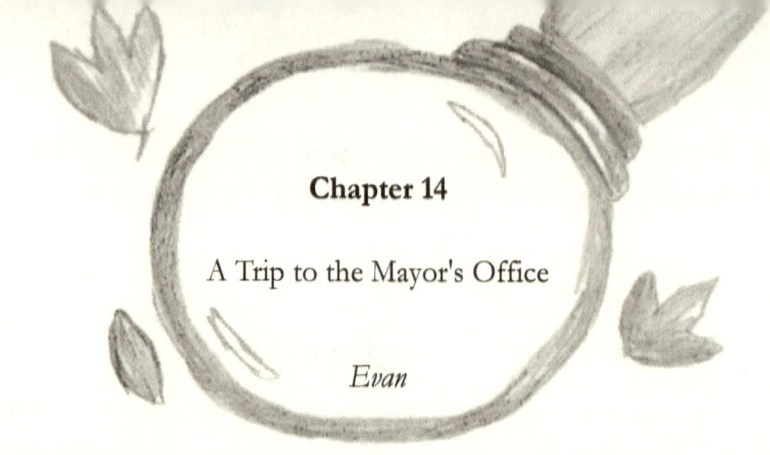

Chapter 14

A Trip to the Mayor's Office

Evan

EVAN CALLED TO Thomas and Brooke, "You guys, the line's moving!" There was only one person in front of him now, and his sister and Thomas were taking forever. Lucky for him, just as he reached the front of the line, they came running back. Clearly, there was something they wanted to tell him.

"Yes, how can I help you?" the receptionist asked, staring at them from across her desk.

"We were wondering if the mayor is in his office," Thomas responded.

"Oh, you're those kids from the other day," the receptionist said, smiling at Brooke and Evan. "Did you want to see your father again?"

"No, we're here to speak with the mayor," Brooke replied, stepping closer to the counter. "It's important, and this is our friend."

"Alright, well, give me just a second to call him," the receptionist replied, picking up the phone.

While she was on the call, Evan whispered, "So, what did you guys find in the seating area?"

He looked up and could see the receptionist setting the phone down.

"We found some footprints," Brooke whispered back. "I'll tell you about it later."

"Sorry, kids, but he's currently speaking with someone. If you want to wait here in the lobby, I'm sure he'll be free soon."

After glancing at Brooke and Thomas, Evan said, "That's too bad. We had something important to talk to him about."

"I'm sorry, the mayor is an important person, and he often has visitors," the receptionist said.

Just as they turned to leave, Brooke asked the receptionist, "Out of curiosity, the mayor didn't happen to speak with Julie Peters before the incident, did he?"

"Actually, yes, he did. He's had many meetings with her and her father before. Now, if you'll please step out of line. There are other people waiting."

"Thank you," Brooke said as she joined Evan and Thomas.

Evan was curious. "Why'd you want to know if the mayor spoke with Julie?"

"Just to see if my suspicion was right," replied Brooke, looking around.

"Here, come on," she said quickly to the boys as she began walking toward the stairs.

"Where are you going?" Evan called after her.

"Not so loud! I'm trying to get to the mayor's office. Are you coming?"

Thomas looked at Evan and then back at Brooke. Quietly, he asked, "Isn't that like illegal or something?"

Brooke quickly responded, "Is what illegal?"

"Sneaking into the mayor's office," Thomas said.

"No, and besides, we're not sneaking *into* the mayor's office; we're sneaking *up to* the mayor's office."

The boys stared at her. "Now, come on," she said.

After a quick glance at each other, Evan and Thomas hurried to follow Brooke up the stairs. Brooke had already made it up the stairs and around the corner, with Thomas right behind her. Evan would have made it, too, if he hadn't tripped. He got up as quickly as he could... just as the receptionist did the same.

She began hurrying over to the stairs and shouting as Evan hurried around the corner and down the hall. Rushing to catch up with the other two, he made a sharp turn around the next corner and nearly crashed into the wall. If it were just the receptionist chasing him, Evan didn't think he would have cared as much. But when he noticed two burly security guards chasing him, too, he didn't want to stick around to see what would happen.

Why is this place so big? Evan frantically thought to himself. He was separated from Thomas and Brooke, and it felt like he was going in circles. Finally, he thought he recognized the door to the mayor's office. *Yes!* He found his sister and friend waiting for him. Brooke waved him over, and a look of confusion and then realization appeared on her face when she saw the security guards behind him.

Still running up to the door, Evan had already decided he wasn't going to wait! He pushed the door open, sending all three teenagers crashing into the room. Rushing up behind them, the security guards grabbed Evan by the arm.

Brooke cried out, turning to her brother, "Evan!"

Before he could respond to his sister, one of the guards spoke to the mayor.

"Sorry about this, Sir. These kids were snooping by your door. Then, this one just came running through the hall, and we had to hurry to stop him. It won't happen again."

"No, that's alright," said Mayor Andrews with a wave of his hand. "I've been wanting to speak with this young lady for a while, actually." He looked directly at Brooke.

Then, the mayor addressed the guards again. "You two are dismissed." They exchanged confused looks with each other and then left the office and went back down the hall.

Standing up and brushing themselves off, the teens stood and looked at the mayor.

"You've been wanting to talk to *me*?" Brooke asked.

"I have," came the mayor's response. "But I assume it's for the same reason you're here—to discuss the case with me?"

"That's right," she responded, looking at Evan and Thomas.

"Then please, all of you have a seat." Mayor Andrews motioned to the chairs around his desk.

After being seated, Evan said to the mayor, "I thought you were already speaking with someone. That's what your receptionist told us."

"Oh, I was. I just finished a conversation before you three showed up," he explained. "A girl by the name of Whitney." The mayor pulled up his own chair and took a seat. He turned his attention to Brooke. "Anyway, you were going to tell me about this mystery of yours?"

"Yes," Brooke responded. Then it dawned on her. "Wait, I'm sorry. Did you say, *Whitney?*"

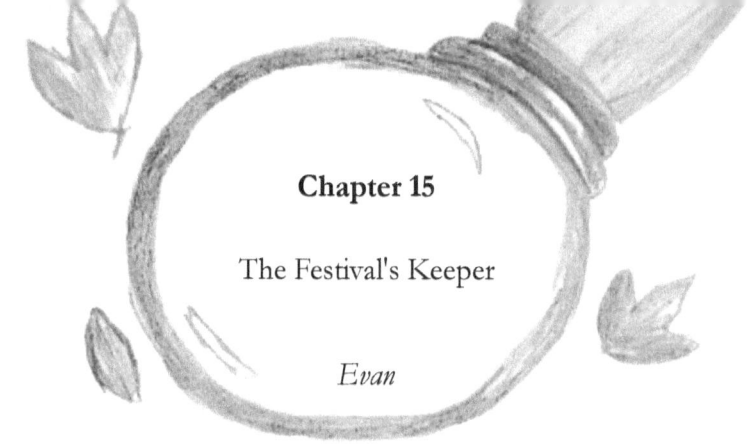

Chapter 15

The Festival's Keeper

Evan

"T HAT'S RIGHT, Whitney Blaire," replied the mayor. "Do you know her?"

"As a matter of fact, we do," Thomas responded.

"Was she talking to you about the case, by chance?" Brooke asked.

"Yes, she was. Actually, she told me she had already solved it, but she wouldn't show me any evidence or give me any proof," the mayor said with a wry smile. "I expect you have better results?"

"Yes, we do," Evan spoke up. "I'm sure my sister can tell you, but first, may I ask you a few questions?"

Mayor Andrews directed his attention to Evan and responded, "Fire away."

"Alright, thank you. The festival really seems to be a hit this year. Did you plan it all yourself?"

Mayor Andrews looked surprised by the question but replied, "Not what I expected you to ask, but I'll answer your question anyway. No, I normally do not manage these major events by myself. Many people usually help out. However, this year, I didn't do any of the planning at all. My daughter did."

"So, this year, she was in charge of everything?" Thomas questioned.

"That's right. She wanted to do it all by herself this year. She loves to bring mindfulness and organization to her projects. This festival means a lot to her. She's attended ever since she was a little girl."

"So, she made all the preparations for the festival?" Evan asked.

"That's right," Mayor Andrews said, nodding.

"Do you think we could talk to her? I have a few questions to ask," Evan said, just as there was a knock on the door.

"I'm currently in a meeting. Who is it?" Mayor Andrews called out as he stood and walked toward the door.

"It's me, Dad!"

The door opened, and Kate stepped in.

"I can come back later if you're busy right now," she said to her father. "I just wanted to talk about a few things regarding the festival."

"No, that's alright. That just so happens to be what we were just talking about."

Mayor Andrews approached his desk and sat back in his chair.

"I believe these young people wanted to speak with you about the festival." The mayor motioned toward them.

Kate noticed Brooke and gave a quick, awkward smile before she took a seat.

"Evan, you had some questions, didn't you?" Mayor Andrews asked.

"Oh, yes, thank you," Evan said. To Kate, he said, "Your father just told us about how you planned everything for the festival this year. Was it harder work than you expected?"

"It was a little complicated, but after I got everything organized, things went smoothly," Kate answered. "Besides that, it was easier than I expected it to be."

"Alright, I think I understand. But you mentioned that the organizing was complicated, right?

"That's right. Why are you asking?"

"If organizing is the main thing, then what was the rest of the planning you mentioned? The part about everything *else* being easier, I mean."

Kate seemed a little distracted. She busied herself with her hair, but she responded to Evan in a confident but slightly disappointed tone. "Well, every year, the festival did pretty well. At least that's how it used to be. Lately, though, fewer people were showing up."

Here, Mayor Andrews spoke up. "Yes, that's right. Lately, there's been a decrease in attendance. Is that all you wanted to ask her?"

Evan opened his mouth to reply, but Kate spoke first. "My dad's right. Over the past two years, attendance has really been slowing down. I actually got lucky this year with so many people showing up." Then she added with a bit of smugness, "Well, with *me* being the one who organized it this year and all."

Brooke jumped in with a question. "Do you have any guesses about why the attendance might have been much higher this year?"

This question seemed to startle Kate, and she took a while before answering. Mayor Andrews looked like he wanted to say something but didn't.

"Well, I guess it might have been because of the incident near the river," Kate said. "Some people must've heard the story and wanted to come see for themselves."

She abruptly stood up and pushed her chair in.

"I'd love to answer more questions for you, but I've actually got to get going now." She started toward the door. "I just remembered that I promised my mother I would be back home soon. I just stopped in to say 'Hi' to my dad."

Evan glanced at his sister before responding. "Alright, well, thank you for your time."

After a quick nod, Kate hurried out the door, leaving them alone with the mayor once again.

They sat in silence for a moment before Mayor Andrews turned his attention back to the others and said, "Sorry about that. She's usually a lot more talkative. This whole festival thing really meant a lot to her, and unfortunately, she doesn't feel she has been doing very well planning it."

"That's alright, Mayor Andrews," Brooke said. "Besides, if Evan's done, I'd like to speak to you about the case now."

"Certainly," Mayor Andrews said. He looked at Evan.

"That's fine with me. I'm done talking," Evan said, turning to his sister. "Go ahead."

Brooke relayed everything to the mayor that they had discovered so far about the case. He listened without asking any questions at all. She thought about adding in her suspicions about how Kate might be involved but knew it would be best to leave that out for now. After all, Kate *was* his daughter.

Seeming to sense that Brooke was thinking about asking something related to Kate, the mayor quickly spoke. "Like I said, I know Kate seemed a little off earlier, but that's just because she's worried about the festival. Once she's feeling a little better about things, I know she'll also be in a better mood."

He got up from his chair, giving them the hint that the meeting was over.

Brooke followed, pushing her chair in as she spoke. "I understand. The festival seems to mean a lot to her."

Mayor Andrews had nothing more to say.

After quick handshakes, Brooke, Evan, and Thomas left the office and walked back down the hall. They were each thinking about the conversation they'd just had with Mayor Andrews and Kate.

As they stepped out into the lobby, Thomas pointed and said, "Hey, you guys, look!"

"What is it?" Brooke asked, looking in the direction he pointed.

Thomas said, "There's nothing there!"

Brooke and Evan looked at each other for a second, bewildered.

"If there's nothing there, then how are we supposed to see something?" Evan asked.

"That's just it!" Thomas said, going to the main area of the lobby. As he stepped onto the oversized white rug, he pointed again. "See, there's nothing there! No muddy footprints anymore, not even on the rug."

"Hey, you're right!" Brooke said, walking over and inspecting the ground. As Thomas and Brooke were looking at where the footprints used to be, Evan came to them with a confused look on his face.

"What are you guys talking about?" He was confused.

"Earlier, while you were in line, Thomas and I found some muddy footprints. There was one on the tile and one on the rug. We never got to tell you!"

Now certain that both footprints were definitely gone, Thomas went to Evan. "You've got a watch, right?"

Still looking confused, Evan held his arm out for Thomas to see his wrist.

"Uh, yeah. Why?" he asked.

"How long do you think we were in the meeting?"

"Well, I don't know exactly what time we got here, but I'd say we were probably there for about half an hour. Why'd you want to know?"

Motioning to the rug, Thomas said, "We were in here thirty minutes ago, and the footprints were there then. Now, they're not."

He paused, having Brooke and Evan's full attention. "Well, it sure didn't take them long to clean up the footprints, did it?"

Chapter 16

The Case Cracked!

Brooke

"YOU KNOW, it just doesn't make sense," Brooke said as they walked out of the mayor's office building.

"What doesn't make sense?" Evan asked his sister.

"This whole thing," she said, motioning around with her hand. "I've got a-fairly good idea of what happened to Julie at the river. But every time I try to piece it together, I can't figure out how the muddy footprints fit in. Or how they got there."

As they walked, she continued to think of possible ways—*any* possible way, those footprints could have gotten there. The ideas she had come up with before didn't seem to work with the case now. As Brooke was thinking things through, she noticed Thomas' face brighten.

"You guys, I just thought of something!" he exclaimed, stopping in the middle of the sidewalk.

"What?" Brooke and Evan both asked, stopping and turning to him.

"It's probably a long shot, but what if the footprints aren't even a part of the mystery?" Thomas said, looking from Brooke to Evan.

After thinking it over for a second, Evan responded, "Well, there's a possibility. But I don't think…"

"Just hear me out," Thomas interrupted. "So, as I was saying, what if the footprints have nothing to do with the case? Someone who came from over by the river could have just stepped there with muddy shoes."

He gestured toward Brooke and added, "Or they could have been there, and you never paid attention to them the first time you were there. While those are both possibilities, the one I'm leaning toward makes more sense," he said, pausing.

After waiting for him to continue, Brooke anxiously asked, "So, what's the one you're leaning toward?"

"Well, it's only a guess, but what if someone put those two footprints there on purpose? Like maybe to throw us off onto the wrong trail."

"Good suggestion," Evan said. "But who would do that?"

"Well, obviously, someone who doesn't want us to solve the case. Not only that, but also, in order to put those muddy footprints there, whoever it was had to know when we were going to be there. They couldn't put them there too soon, or they'd get mopped up early. They couldn't be late either, or we wouldn't see them," Thomas explained. He waited, hoping to see that the other two understood what he was saying.

"That being said, they must have literally done it once they saw us walking up to the building," he continued. "Then, they hurried to put down the footprints. But by then, we'd be entering the building, which means they wouldn't be able to avoid being seen by us, but they wouldn't be able to exit the building either. That means whoever it was would have still been in the building when we got there." Thomas finished and waited for their reactions.

"Whitney!" Brooke exclaimed.

Both boys turned to her as she went on. "She was still in the building when we got there, in a meeting with the mayor. The mayor said that once we arrived at his office, she had just left—possibly to avoid being seen." Brooke paused for a moment, trying to recall more information, then she continued.

"When I first met with her, she got upset when I told her I was solving the case. She made it clear that *she* wanted to be the one to solve it, which would explain the muddy footprints because she must have been investigating down by the river. Finally, I bet she put those two footprints there on purpose by bringing along an extra pair of shoes, sticking them in the mud, and then bringing them into the lobby to throw us off. That way, *she* would get the credit for solving the case!" She triumphantly turned to Evan and Thomas.

"I figured it was Whitney," Thomas replied excitedly. "I just didn't know how yet, but your conclusion makes sense!"

"Wait. You said you've already figured out the case, right?" Evan asked Brooke.

"That's right," she happily replied.

"Then what are we waiting for? Let's go tell the mayor!" Evan said excitedly as he motioned toward the mayor's office.

Brooke was excited, too, but she hesitated. "Wait. I think we should call him first and request another meeting. We can ask for Whitney and Kate to be there as well." Brooke said.

The boys nodded in agreement. Brooke took the lead, and they began walking again. In her mind, she ran through what she would say to the mayor. She ended with a final thought to herself: *This should be interesting!*

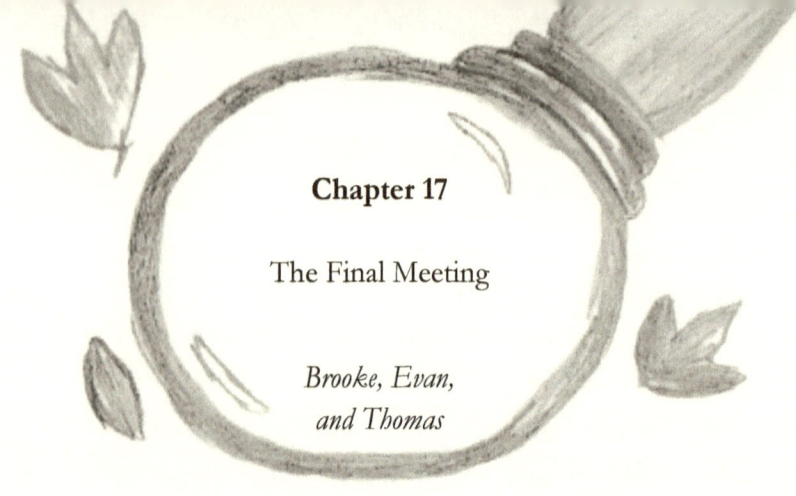

Chapter 17

The Final Meeting

Brooke, Evan,
and Thomas

"EXCUSE ME, we need to speak with the mayor," Brooke said as she stepped up to the counter to wait for the receptionist, who was busy at her computer. She looked up, typed a few seconds longer, and then came to the counter where Brooke, Evan, and Thomas stood.

"Oh, you three are the kids who came in here before. Are you back to see the mayor again?" She eyed them suspiciously.

Nodding, Brooke responded, "Yep, and it's kinda important. Is he available?"

"He might be," the receptionist said and stepped over to her desk to call the mayor's office. While talking, she kept a close eye on the group in front of her. Once she finished the call, she walked back to Brooke.

"He said he's expecting you. You can go up and speak with him…" She paused, turned, and pointed to Evan, "But no funny business this time!"

Evan gave an embarrassed smile, and then the two boys followed Brooke up the stairs to the mayor's office. As they went down the hall, they passed by the security officers, who glared at them as they walked by.

"You'd think *I* was the culprit in the case," Evan whispered to the other two as they passed the officers.

"That would be an interesting story," Brooke said.

"What?" Evan asked.

"A story where the detective and her friends are the culprits—I don't think there's a story like that yet."

"Probably because then there wouldn't be a story or anything to solve," Thomas said as they rounded the corner. "The detective would already know what happened because *she* committed the crime."

"I guess you're right," replied Brooke. "It would've been interesting, though."

"Well, let's not let *that* story happen," Evan said. He glanced at his sister and then quickly back at the officers.

As their discussion ended, they reached the door of the mayor's office.

Turning to look at her friend and her brother, Brooke asked, "Are you guys ready to solve our first case?" She was clearly excited!

Thomas responded first, "You bet we are! We've been waiting for the big reveal, and now we get to hear it!"

Brooke looked at Evan next, and he nodded. "Yeah! I can't wait to see their faces when they find out who the culprit is!"

"Or culprits," Thomas added.

The door to the mayor's office swung open just as they approached. The mayor stood there in front of them.

"Oh, there you are. I was wondering when you were going to get here." He looked at each of them in turn. "The receptionist told me you were on your way."

Mayor Andrews stepped back from the doorway and motioned for them to come in. "Alright," he said. "You can begin whenever you're ready."

Everyone stared expectantly at Brooke.

"I assume you've cracked the case. Isn't that why we're all here?" Mayor Andrews asked, gesturing around with his hands at the people she had invited.

Brooke smiled and looked first at Evan, then at Thomas. Finally, she looked directly at the mayor.

"Yes, I have, Mayor Andrews, and you are *not* going to believe me when I tell you what *really* happened."

Chapter 18

The Culprit Exposed

Brooke

A FTER EVERYONE HAD taken their seats, Brooke looked around the table and took in the seating arrangement. The table was oval-shaped, and she and the mayor were seated at the ends. On the left side of the table sat Thomas and Kate. On the right were Evan and Whitney.

Brooke noticed right away that Kate seemed nervous. She was constantly fidgeting with her hands under the table. Whitney seemed to be annoyed and was busy on her phone, although that, of course, was what she normally did. The mayor looked rather serious, and both Thomas and Evan were eager for the meeting to start.

"Now that we're all comfy, why don't you begin?" Mayor Andrews said a bit sarcastically.

Brooke had been waiting for this moment since she started the case, and now she didn't know where to begin. Everyone was staring at her, so she knew she had to start with something. Putting her hands together on the table, dramatically, she started speaking.

"I'll begin with the start of this case, when we first showed up here in New York." Brooke looked around at the faces staring back at her. "But before I do, I want you to know you're all here for a reason. Each of you has something to do with this case." Here, she paused and looked across the table at the mayor. "Including you, Mayor Andrews," she said.

Brooke swiftly recalled all the events of the case in her mind before she continued. "Now, I'll begin. I'd say this probably started when I picked up the newspaper. It didn't seem right that no one ever found Julie Peters alive or recovered her body. If I know my geography, which I do, then the Bloomington River hits a piece of land before it makes it to the ocean. That piece of land is rather large, and I find it very odd that no one could find her body there unless they didn't look— or unless the body isn't there. If she went downstream, her body would *have* to be there because the flow of the water would be stopped by the land."

"Well, how could the body *not* be there?" Whitney questioned. "I mean, you just got done telling us that..."

"I just finished telling you that the body would have had to hit land, I know. Unless... it never made it down the river in the first place."

"The article said that the girl fell into the river. She would have had to go downstream," Whitney said hotly, rather annoyed by being cut off by Brooke.

"That's correct. Well, part of it is anyway," Brooke said. "I have reason to believe that she went *into* the water but never went downstream."

Whitney opened her mouth to speak again, but she changed her mind and remained silent. Brooke figured she was trying to come up with something to make her conclusion backfire but couldn't think of anything.

No one else spoke, so Brooke continued. "I believe Julie was *pushed* in, but not because someone was angry with her.

Instead, I have reason to believe she knew she was going to be pushed, and she actually planned it."

With this, she focused her full attention on Kate. Under Brooke's gaze, Kate promptly looked away and once more busied herself with her hair.

"Kate, I was passing by on my way back to the lobby when I overheard a conversation going on between you and two of your father's security officers. So, you have authority over the officers, too? Wow."

Kate began to speak, but the mayor jumped in first. "She helps me out with a lot of things around here, including the festival this year, which we spoke of previously. My security staff was in charge of the river near the festival, so yes, Kate was in charge of them, too."

"Okay, thank you, Mayor Andrews." Brooke was still looking at Kate, who was avoiding any eye contact. "Well, during that conversation, she told them that they were absolutely *not* allowed to investigate near the river. At the time, I figured it was to avoid drawing crowds over to the river. One reason is because it's so easy to fall in." She shot a quick glance at Evan.

Brooke continued, "But I discovered that wasn't the reason because when my brother and I went to the river, a security officer was sent to our house to find out why we were in that area.

"While this could have been just to see if we were alright, I doubt it. Why, you might ask? Two reasons. First, because he said he saw Evan almost fall into the river. But while we were there, there weren't any security officers around the entire festival area. Second, he must have been hiding by the river in order for him to know we were there without us knowing *he* was there."

Brooke kept speaking clearly and confidently. "Along with this, we also know who was in charge of that officer and who wanted them *not* to be publicly noticeable by the river."

Kate seemed to shrink down in her chair a little, but after a sharp glance from her father, she sat up straight again.

"I don't like how you're *only* talking about my daughter," Mayor Andrews said, glaring across the table at Brooke.

Brooke held his gaze. "Oh no, Mayor Andrews. I'm not finished explaining it all to you yet."

He settled himself back in his seat and waited for her to continue.

"Now, I understand this festival meant a lot to Kate because she's been going since she was little. Isn't that right, Kate?" Brooke asked.

For once, Kate confidently made eye contact with Brooke. "That's right," she said. "I've gone every year for as long as I can remember."

Nodding, Brooke continued. "Okay, thank you. Now, I'll move on to another aspect of the case. I spoke with a few local people around the area who claimed to have known Julie. Most said she was known for acting and singing, and she always loved to get attention. One person told me that Julie occasionally put on plays with her parents for the entire town."

Looking across the table at the mayor, Brooke asked, "Was Julie a good actress?"

"I suppose. I remember Kate always liked to attend her shows," Mayor Andrews replied, the same serious expression remaining on his face.

"Oh, so you and Kate have gone to Julie's shows before?" Brooke asked curiously.

He gave a brief nod. "That's right."

Whitney interrupted impatiently. "Are you ready to reveal who did it yet?"

"Just about," Brooke responded as she prepared to finish up. "First, I'll go over what we just talked about," she said. Whitney gave an exaggerated roll of her eyes.

Ignoring her, Brooke said, "So, Kate has control over your security officers. Julie was a singer and actress. Julie put on plays, and Kate and Mayor Andrews went to some of her plays. That about sums it up."

Brooke looked around at everyone; they were all staring at her. Standing up, she brought her speech to a close. "Now, you've been waiting all this time, wanting to know who the culprit is, I'm sure." She hesitated, making it a point to look at each person around the table.

"So, then I'll have no trouble revealing to you that it is…."

With this, she slammed both hands down on the table dramatically and then pointed.

"Kate!" Brooke exclaimed.

Chapter 19

The Big Reveal

Brooke

K ATE WORE A SHOCKED expression as everyone in the room turned their attention to her.

"Me?" she questioned innocently.

"That's right, and I believe your father's in on it, too," Brooke said, turning to Mayor Andrews. "Kate clearly cared about the festival, which made you care about it, too. She convinced you to let her organize the festival this year, and you agreed."

Mayor Andrews glared back at her.

"By being able to do that, she then had authority over the security officers as well. She kept them from investigating near the river, with the appearance of keeping people away from it so no one else would fall in. But she also wanted the attendance rate to go up, as she mentioned to me the other day, which she also just confirmed here today. She's been trying to make sure things don't decline even more *this* year, so she had to find a way to make more people show up!"

"That doesn't exactly make sense, though," Thomas said. He turned to Brooke. "I understand what you're saying, but what's wrong with her wanting a boost in attendance?"

"Yeah, who pushed Julie in, or did she fall in?" Whitney asked, looking over at Brooke.

"Kate did!" Brooke exclaimed.

Again, everyone turned to look at Kate. Her expression changed from innocent to serious and, finally, annoyed.

"Alright, fine! I pushed her in," she admitted. "But that's not the full story!"

"That's right," Brooke said, as everyone stared at Kate in surprise. "It's *not* the full story. Kate pushed Julie into the river, knowing that she wouldn't be washed downstream. The whole thing was planned!" Brooke said, looking around at them all as she spoke.

"Kate figured that if something dramatic or mysterious happened near the festival, it would create interest. It would be covered by the media, and people would be curious, and therefore, more people would show up. She was exactly right, too, and as Thomas was saying, it boosted the attendance."

Kate was quiet. She sat with her head down and fidgeting hands in her lap.

"We already knew Julie was an actress, so why wouldn't it make sense that Kate paid her to act and let herself be pushed into the river?

"Good point, but why would she do that?" Evan asked.

"As I was just saying, she wanted to *up* the attendance. Not many people showed up at the festival last year. The festival is special to her, and she didn't want it to end, so she got more people to show up."

Brooked turned to Kate and asked, "Am I right, Kate?"

Kate nodded slowly and looked up at Brooke. "You're right, but I don't quite understand how you figured it out so well."

Brooke smiled victoriously before responding. "I'm just good at what I do."

Mayor Andrews looked genuinely shocked. Until that moment, Brooke hadn't been sure if he had known what his daughter had been up to.

Mayor Andrew turned to Kate, clearly disappointed. "I knew you were up to something, but I never would've guessed *this*." Piecing things together himself, the mayor continued, "Kate, how could you use that little girl like that?"

Kate looked at her father. "Well, I realize now that it was pretty bad, but at the time, I just wanted to attract more people to the festival. Dad, you knew how important it was to me. It's been my special place ever since I was a little girl… like Julie."

"Still, Kate, you should have talked to me. We could've run an ad or a story in the newspaper or something—so more people would know about it."

Mayor Andrews seemed to realize the irony of his words. He paused, looked at his daughter, and gave a slight, sad chuckle. "But I guess you already did that," he joked half-heartedly. There was an uneasy silence as everyone let the new information settle in.

Then Whitney spoke up. "So, why am *I* here?" she asked, rather annoyed. "Did you just call me here to say *you* solved the case, and I didn't?"

Brooke turned to Whitney. "Not exactly, although I *was* hoping I'd be able to solve the case first," she said with a smile.

Whitney rolled her eyes yet again. "*You're* here for another matter," Brooke said.

"Oh, the footprints! Right?" Thomas asked.

"That's right!" Brooke replied. "Whitney, you come into this case not as a culprit but as someone who was trying to mislead us."

"You don't have any proof of that," Whitney said, staring angrily at her.

"Actually, I do." Brooke now addressed the group. "She tried to mislead us with the muddy footprints."

"I don't know what you're talking about," Whitney replied innocently.

This time, it was Brooke who rolled her eyes. "You placed two footprints in the lobby, and I'm going to explain how I know it was you."

The mayor gestured for her to continue, and after a moment, she did so.

"When I first met you, you got upset when I told you I was trying to solve the case, and you said *you* wanted to be the one to solve it. Since then, you've been trying to solve it before I could." As Brooke was speaking, she noticed Whitney glaring at her, obviously irritated.

"To figure out more about the case, we stopped by her mom's clothing store, and she made sure to say that she had already solved the case. Later on, though, when I spoke with Mayor Andrews, he told me Whitney said she *had* solved it but didn't give any proof."

Whitney interrupted. "It's a *boutique*, not a clothing store! Also, what does this have to do with the case?"

"I wasn't finished speaking," Brooke said. *She* was rather annoyed now. "Plus, if you'd let me finish, you'd find out a lot sooner."

This quieted Whitney, and she stopped talking.

"Now, as I was saying," Brooke said, eyeing Whitney. Seeing she wouldn't be interrupted again, she continued. "The last time we came here to speak with the mayor, we discovered two footprints. Now we know how the lobby is always kept very neat, so these muddy footprints seemed very much out of place. They didn't stay there long, though, because once we finished speaking with the mayor, they were gone.

"Along with that, two questions remained. We wondered how they got there and who left them. After considering this for a while, we discovered whoever it was had to still be in the building. There was no other way for them to know what time we'd be there so the footprints would be seen before they were cleaned up. They also had to still be in the building, just like Whitney was in the building, in a meeting with Mayor Andrews at that exact time.

"Finally, you had been investigating down near the river to try to solve the case before me, which means your shoes must have gotten muddy. It hasn't rained for days, so that was an easy one to figure out. You swapped shoes but took them with you to place the footprints in the lobby and throw us off."

With that, Brooke finished speaking and took a deep breath. The whole case was unraveled, and everyone was taking in what was just said. Now the culprit was revealed, and everyone was slowly turning their attention from Kate to Whitney and then back to Brooke.

"So, where is Julie, then?" Evan asked Kate. "You know they've already set up a date for her funeral, right?"

Kate glanced around nervously. "Actually, I heard about that. Julie was just going to show up randomly tomorrow and resume things as normal. Her parents were fine with it. They thought it would be great for her future acting career. Once people got over the fact that she wasn't dead, things would go back to how they were."

"Are you saying you were never going to tell anybody what really happened?" Whitney asked. "So, for the rest of her life, people would just think she'd been a ghost for a few days? Really?"

"I would have told them, eventually," Kate said. "It was just delayed… for dramatic effect."

"Wow, you are really something," Thomas said. "*You're* the real actress here."

Brooke added, "Well, I hope you would have told the truth either way."

"Now things will go back to normal. Right?" Evan asked. "You *are* gonna tell them everything?"

Mayor Andrews interrupted. "Yes! We'll tell everyone, including the media, what happened. We'll issue a statement and link it to Julie's wonderful acting skills, a publicity stunt for the festival, or practice for an upcoming play, or… something like that!" The mayor threw up his hands, clearly frustrated and upset.

"Yes, Dad," Kate agreed. But *I* need to be the one to tell it."

She turned to Brooke with pleading eyes. "Brooke, just do me one favor. Please don't tell anybody yet. *I* want to be the one to do the big reveal, so to speak—even if it's not a good one." She sounded tearful.

"Probably more dramatics," Thomas mumbled.

Brooke actually felt sorry for Kate. This was a big mess to clean up. *I wouldn't want to be her*, she thought.

"Alright. We'll keep quiet for now," Brooke agreed. "Just make sure you give a true statement tomorrow morning. Okay?"

"Yes, okay," Kate said. "I will. Thank you."

Chapter 20

The Young Master Detectives

Brooke

"**D**O YOU GUYS have to go back?" Thomas asked Evan as he helped him bring suitcases out to the car.

Evan set the bag he was carrying down by the trunk. "Yeah. We've got school and stuff to get back to."

"It'd be cool if you guys could stay, though. It was fun solving the mystery with you," Thomas said. He put the suitcases down next to Evan's bag.

"Well, knowing my sister, we'll be solving another mystery soon enough," Evan joked.

As if on cue, Brooke came out, lugging her dark blue suitcase, and joined them. "Dad says we're about ready to go." Turning to Thomas, she said, "It was fun solving the mystery with you."

"I agree," Thomas said, smiling. Then his expression changed as an idea popped into his head. "Hey, we should come up with a cool name for ourselves since we're officially detectives now," he suggested, looking over at Brooke and Evan.

"Hey, good idea!" Brooke responded.

"How about *The Three Detecteers*?" Evan suggested.

Both Brooke and Thomas gave him a confused look.

"What's a detecteer?" Thomas asked.

"You know, like *The Three Musketeers*? Well, if you combine detective and musketeer, then you get *detecteer*," Evan explained.

No response.

After a moment, he said, "You know, it sounded a lot better in my head."

There was a brief silence as the three of them tried to come up with a name. Then, Thomas spoke up. "I know! How about *The Master Detectives*?"

"I like it," Evan said. "But what about The *Young Master Detectives*? Typically, older people do the sleuthing. That way, we'd be different!"

"Oh wait, I think I've got something too!" He continued. "Brooke, remember that thing you said when Kate asked you how you solved the case?"

"Um, I think so. Wasn't it… I'm just good at what I do?"

"Yeah, that's what it was!"

"Hey, we can have a motto too!" Thomas exclaimed. "The Young Master Detectives—we're just good at what we do."

"I think that sounds pretty good," Evan said.

"Me too!" Brooke agreed.

"Alrighty, then! *The Young Master Detectives*, it is!" Thomas said.

They all high-fived just as Brooke and Evan's dad came out with the last suitcase.

"Alright, kids. Ready to go?" he asked. They both said, "Yes," and opened the car doors.

"Hey, you guys!" Thomas called. "Just a second!"

Brooke and Evan turned to see Thomas holding out his phone.

"Let's exchange numbers," Thomas explained. "So that way, we can all keep in touch, and you can let me know if you find another mystery that needs solving."

"Alright, when another one happens, we'll let you know," Brooke responded.

After sharing their numbers, she and Evan got in the car. As their dad drove away, they waved at Thomas until he climbed onto his bike and rode away.

Brooke could barely believe it. She had just cracked her first case!

As they began passing by buildings once more, there was one recurring thought in her mind. *Young Master Detective Brooke Alans.*

She thought, *I like the sound of that!*

Acknowledgments

I'm very grateful and would like to thank my mom for standing by me throughout the entire process of getting this book published. She worked super hard and did a bunch of behind-the-scenes work (sometimes very late at night) to get this book where it is now. So, thank you, Mom!

Thank you to my Grandpa for encouraging me and telling me to keep writing. Thanks as well to my brothers, who read the whole book through and critiqued me as I went along. Thank you to my six-month-old niece, who sat and watched me write, and also pterodactyl screamed at random times (I appreciate all your helpful advice.) And a big thanks to all my friends and family who said they couldn't wait to read this book. You don't know how much that made me smile.

I'd also like to thank my publishing coaches, Shana Danielle and Nicole Donoho with ThriveIn Learning Institute, for hanging in there and answering my book questions, and taking their time to explain things thoroughly even when my brain stopped working. A big thanks to my editor, Naomi V. Dunsen-White, and proofreader, LuAnne Gilchrist, from Naomi Books, LLC.

Thanks to Kanwal with ThriveIn Learning Institute, for their amazing cover design. It really makes the book's suspenseful and intriguing aspects stand out; you exceeded my expectations! It was definitely not what I expected it to look like, and every bit exactly how I wanted it to be!

Finally, I want to thank any reader who happened along and picked up this book. Thank you so much for joining me on this journey into the detective world! It's crazy to think that the majority of people reading this book will be only a few years younger than me! Crazy right? Well, from a kid to a kid, I hope you enjoy this book and have fun solving the mystery!

About the Author

Sarah Rivera, an aspiring mystery and detective author from Oklahoma, began writing books for children and pre-teens at the young age of 15. She loves to create stories with compelling, captivating, and suspenseful plots, full of twists and turns, to always keep you on the edge of your seat.

Photo credit to: Natalie Maher

In her debut book, *The Case Files of Young Master Detective Brooke Alans: The Mysterious Disappearance at Bloomington River*, readers get to take a look inside the captivating world of sleuthing in order to find out what happened to young Julie Peters and why she went missing in the first place.

Sarah Rivera has always loved storytelling with a special passion for writing mystery books, short stories, riddles, and songs. When she's not writing, you'll find her singing, playing violin and piano, acting, drawing, and spending time with her family and cats. She believes the reason she's been able to discover so many talents and has achieved so many different skills is because she lives by the belief that she can do anything she puts her mind to… and then does just that! Sarah hopes that by her example, you'll see that even at a young age, you can accomplish great things, too!

Stay connected with the author! Scan the QR code below and follow @SarahRivera on Facebook and @sarahriveraauthor on Instagram for updates on her upcoming works!

www.ingramcontent.com/pod-product-compliance
Lightning Source LLC
Chambersburg PA
CBHW030653110726
47901CB00002B/699